A horrific and disturbing violent assault amidst a straightforward drug deal creates tension between the powerful and dangerous Bakker and Volvov families.

Who is The Apparition, is he a small-time incompetent criminal or an accomplished assassin, and master of disguise?

The Devil has reappeared after two decades and is now on the hunt of The Apparition, the terror of The Dutchman has returned.

Will Isla's inheritance be the death of her?

Can a mistaken identity lead to an innocent man being framed for crimes that he did not commit?

Michael Craig

Doppelgänger

Harbinger of Evil

To Victoria

I wish I'd met you before, I should have waited for you.

Now that you are here, I hope that you will stay a while. Cx

And to Archie,

you were with us for only a short time, you broke all the rules, and you taught us to chill the 'F' out.

Prologue

Die

(Kyle)

Will no one rid me of this troublesome wife?

I would welcome just one volunteer from a modern-day version of, William de Tracey, Hugh de Morville, Richard le Breton, and Reginal FitzUrse, to be my assassin.

King Henry II had a similar dilemma as I face, an ongoing dispute. His was with the head of the Church of England, over land, power, and taxes. The removal of the Archbishop of Canterbury, Thomas Becket, gave it all to the crown.

My dispute is with my wife, she holds the power, she has cash and assets recently acquired by inheritance and a healthy insurance policy.

I don't have obedient assassins to carry out my murderous orders.

I would do it myself; I think I would take great delight in seeing her life ebb away at my hand, let her see that it was me taking her last breath from her, the last person she sees in her mortal form is that of her husband that she despises and disrespects so much.

Getting away with the perfect murder, is the goal, I am not sure that there is a perfect murder, I would suggest to you that the margins of getting caught are associated with not making that terrible mistake, the foolish error or worse, your arrogance gets the best of you, and you give yourself away.

The Menendez brothers, Erik, and Lyle did not commit the perfect murder, they were caught due their arrogant behaviour.

They bought guns, they used those guns to kill their parents and accused the mafia. They gained to inherit $90 million and had no solid alibi for the time of the murders.

Means, motive, and opportunity, right there.

This was far from perfect, yet the Police did not originally think it was them, they did not search their car for guns, which they would have found. They did not arrest them and take their clothes for forensic examination, nor did they check their hands for gun residue. They had motive and opportunity but were not prime suspects. They had committed the most heinous of crimes but had seemingly, literally, got away with murder.

Their foolish mistake was, that they talked about the murder to an unscrupulous shrink, with a flappy jaw, who intended to extort them. They wrote a play about boys killing their parents and they embarked on an incredible extravagant spending spree instead of keeping a low profile.

OJ Simpson escaped prison for the sloppy, but violent murder of his ex-wife and a waiter, who was in the wrong place at the wrong time, returning a pair of glasses to her address.

He had clear motive and opportunity.

When a spouse or ex-spouse is murdered the husband should expect to be a suspect, in this case OJ had previously made threats to kill her, and he was in the immediate area at the time of the murders.

If, not if, but when Isla is murdered my alibi needs to be watertight.

There was considerable evidence against OJ, that this was not the perfect murder either. Yet he escaped justice because the Jury was hand selected by the defence team, and the prosecution were arrogant about the importance of jury selection. The prosecution made critical errors believing that they had a compelling case, while the defence focussed on persuading the jury that there was reasonable doubt. Asserting that the LAPD were guilty of misconduct relating to racism and incompetence. OJ's defence team succeeded and OJ got away with murder.

He may have escaped prison, but a civil case found him guilty, and he was sued for all his wealth.

That will not work for me, money is my motivation.

I have considered hiring someone to do the killing but, involving others gets you caught.

There are far too many examples of both men and women who have tried to hire a contract killer to bump off someone, they invariable get caught due to intercepted communication or money trails and Police stings.

When a hitman is caught, they almost immediately confess to being a killer for hire and strike a deal for a lenient sentence in exchange for information relating to the person who hired them. I would not trust anyone to be competent enough to get the job done or keep it quiet.

A hitman is not a viable option. Plus, I have no means to raise the money required for such a deal.

The ideal situation would be if someone had a similar appearance to me, then I could be in two places at once, the perfect alibi.

Multiple witnesses to prove I was at that event, that party, a face in the crowd, while the genuine me was carrying out a calculated murder that would reward me with freedom and financial security.

With Isla out of the way, everything will be mine.

Part One
Amsterdam

Calamity Jane

(Kirk)

"Please remain seated until the aeroplane has made a complete stop, and the pilot has switched off the seat belt signs" the automatic announcement message instructed us.

There were a few screams and gasps as the plane hit the runway, hard.

The last 20 minutes of the 55-minute flight, were mostly in silence following the captain briefing, he had advised us that due to high winds at Schiphol airport, the plane's computer would be landing the City Hopper flight from Leeds, "so expect some bumps" he had said.

Having booked my flight late I was not sat with the rest of our party, I was at the very rear of the plane in the window seat, with two girls from somewhere between Halifax and

Huddersfield, Seed-Hall, it sounded like. I googled it later, but I couldn't find a place by that name.

Lucy, who sat next to me on the flight, and Rebecca, who preferred to be called either Becky or Bex, held the aisle seat were entertaining company, the stories they told had me in fits of laughter, I don't believe them all to be true, but they were funny stories.

Lucy told me the story of the local taxi driver in their town that everybody knew as Manny, a man in his late fifties at least. He had been driving all his working life, forty years. His first job after leaving school was as a van driver delivering carpets, then as a Pop Man, yes delivering fizzy drinks, and then he had worked as a Drayman for a local brewery.

Manny, Manvir, to give him his full name had been a taxi driver for only a couple of years, but he kept forgetting that he was a taxi driver.

Every time a passenger would touch his shoulder or talk to him from the rear of the car it would give him a fright. His previous driving job for the past 20 years being that of a funeral car driver.

The locals would stay quiet for long periods of time and when they believed he had forgotten he was taxi driver they would do something to illicit his frightened reaction.

There were multiple stories of Lucy crashing her car, actually her mum's car, and one vehicle related incident involving an unfortunate accident with a Policemen.

Her first crash was the same day she had passed her driving test. She was given the keys of the car by her proud mum, and gleefully set off waving eagerly as she drove off their street turning right past the local farm where she was confronted by a cow that had escaped the field, instead of stopping she had swerved around the animal but had misjudged the distance and drove through a fence into a neighbour's garden.

Her dad spent the weekend rebuilding the fence and replacing the lawn.

Her second escapade occurred when her parents were on holiday, and she had the use of their car. Showing off with three friends in the car they headed into the town centre for a spot of lunch. Rather than attempt to parallel park she decided to park in the supermarket carpark and located a space that was not occupied, and with other cars circling searching for a space she drove at speed into the gap, only to find it was not a parking space. But only after she had collided heavily with a concrete column holding up the roof of the car park.

A new car had been purchased by her parents and an instruction for her to take more care, because the insurance premiums had been increased significantly. She had assured them that accidents were behind her, and she had learned her lessons the hard way.

She carefully reversed the car off the drive with her parents watching on from the passenger side, however she had failed to close the driver's door which was removed from its hinges by the garden wall as she exited the driveway.

By this point I had tears rolling down my face and my cheeks hurt from laughing. When Becky declared that I'd not heard the best of it yet.

By this point Lucy had been given the nickname, Calamity Jane, by her entire family and banned from driving the family car. Instead, she was provided with her own car by her uncle, an older car.

The logbook ownership list read, one careful owner. The car was now doomed.

First, Lucy had tried to turn the car around in the road using an opening between a wall, only to drive off a four-foot ledge and landed on a boulder with all four wheels off the ground.

Another uncle was summoned to rescue her with his truck and a winch.

Next, she crashed the car head on into a concrete step, folding the sub frame, making the vehicle look like an animation from the film Cars.

Her next car was even older with old style window openings with a crank handle, not that they worked, and the windows were sealed permanently shut. This didn't pose a problem until one day when she had accidentally passed through a red light had been followed by a Police car. The Police car immediately illuminated the blue flashing lights and initiated the sirens.

Lucy pulled over and waited for the Policeman to walk to her car. The officer tapped on her driver's side window and motioned for her to wind it down so that he could speak with her. Aware that the window winder didn't work, she panicked and opened the car door instead, just as the officer bent down toward the window, the weight of the door connecting with his temple knocked him out cold on the pavement, with the other Police officer scurrying back to the car to call for back up.

She did evade an endorsement for running the red light, the Policeman who witnessed the infringement was being taken away on a gurney into a nearby ambulance unable to provide a witness statement.

I couldn't take any more car crash stories; my sides were hurting.

I decided I quite liked Lucy, perfect and imperfect in equal measures. She can laugh at herself and doesn't take herself too seriously. I liked that quality.

I was beginning to enjoy the trip, which I hadn't anticipated I would. I had agreed to join the trip at the last minute, I wasn't sure that I'd be in the squad much the coming season and had pretty much decided that this would be my last season of football at this level.

We had won our division title for the past two seasons and many of the players had moved on or retired making way for a more youthful looking team, with designs on being promoted three times in a row or being spotted by a scout and going pro.

Not me, I was one of two in the squad at the end of their football adventure, Big Sam, our goalie, and me, defender come holding midfielder.

I'd been contemplating hanging up my boots in lieu of the inevitable call from the gaffer to have that chat. I'd decided that I would go when the time was right and not wait to be told I no longer fit in the plans.

It was the kit man, Geoff, a gem of a fella, widely respected and liked, not just within our club, but through the entire footballing community, that had called to say that he had not received my passport details and confirmation that I had booked my flight, and that I had better them to him and effin pronto.

I didn't tell him I was thinking of quitting the team, I booked my flight and here I was.

As the plane approached its dock it became clear that the squad had made use of the refreshment trolley and I began to question the sanity of my decision to join, what would be a 3-day bender in Amsterdam, with a few training sessions and a friendly match to make the trip look legit.

Thick as shit

(Bex)

I am not a fan of a guy in a tracksuit, I thought to myself, but Kirk looks, well, fine. Although, he doesn't look particularly comfortable over there with the rest of his football buddies in their matching attire waiting for their luggage at the carousel.

University educated, single, has his own business, car, and owns his own house in Leeds. Vastly different from the boys I know in Halifax. Oh, and drop dead gorgeous too I had commented to Lucy. I had not realised just how big and tall he was on the plane, he stands towering over the rest of his teammates, he must be six foot four or five and has the build of a rugby player rather than a footballer.

My brother is a rugby player for our local club in Siddal, he is thick as shit.

I imagine the other tall fella over there with the team is the goalkeeper, not as athletic looking, long arms and big hands, goalkeeper physique.

I wonder whether Kirk will text me.

The boys in Maroon

(Lucy)

Stop staring Bex, I cannot believe you gave him your telephone number before we got off the plane. I was the one sat next to him, I was the one chatting with him, it was me he is interested in, I wanted to say, but I did not. I never do.

I had established with Kirk, that we were on the same plane home and therefore I was playing it cool, letting him do the chasing, plus I had let it slip which hotel we were staying at in Amsterdam.

We were staying at the hotel Ibis, near the central railway station, conveniently the team were staying at a hostel called Hotel Jimmy on the same street as the Ibis, on Martelaarsgracht. I had joked that he should drop into our hotel bar for a drink, and he said that he would, and that a night with me would be preferable to a night with the lads.

It might not have been said exactly like that, not as direct as that, but I had the impression he would like to have a drink with me.

I felt a connection between us, he shared some intimate details about himself, oh lord, had I pried too much?

He told me that he had been adopted at birth and that one or both of his biological parents were rich or that their families were rich. Rich enough to ensure that there was no record of his official birth, and that he was an unwanted child.

Although he was unwanted, someone wanted him to have a privileged life and education and a trust fund was set up for him, which whenever he or the parents that adopted him needed money this could be accessed through his trustee, Mr Castel.

Mr Castel would make the arrangements, no questions asked.

He attended a private school in Edinburgh, called St George's. It stuck me that this must have been a very English feeling school. He'd attended from age three to eighteen and said that he could have boarded there but that his parents preferred him to be at home, and they did not live far from the school.

He was aware that his parents were provided with the house and an annual allowance from his biological parents via Mr Castel, and he suspected that the allowance was conditional on him living with them, and that if he'd boarded at the school, that they would have lost the house and the allowance.

He'd said that he didn't have a particularly loving childhood, he was a business transaction for his adopted parents, they didn't love him or show any affection, and he didn't like them very much. They had nice things, the house, a car each, they hadn't needed to work, but both had part time jobs as far as he could work out. He'd guessed that this was in readiness for when the income from his adoption would stop. He had stumbled across some bank statements around his eighteenth Birthday that showed a considerable bank balance, and when he asked what they were saving for they had a said "a rainy day". But had warned him that he would not see any of that money and there was no inheritance or anything for him in their wills.

When you leave here, you leave with the clothes on your back, and you are on your own from there on in they'd said, and he knew they'd be true to their word. But that is how he wanted it to be too.

After his A-levels, he'd attended university in Leeds and gained a degree in Sports Science. He could have studied a subject more academic, but it was sport and fitness that he loved.

While he was at university in Leeds, he'd rented a flat above row of shops, from an elderly fellow Scotsman, imaginatively known in the area as, Scotch Bob, although

Kirk said that he like to be called Rab or Rabby.

He and Rabby had become friends despite the age difference, and they had spent many evenings together at Rabby's local pub, the Travellers Rest, and at Rabby's house playing cards or watching sport on TV.

When Rabby died suddenly and without any living relatives, Kirk had been surprised to find that the house and the building with two empty shops and the flat above had been left to him in Rabby's will.

This, as it turned out, had been rather fortunate for Kirk as a few months later after he had turned twenty-one years of age and graduated from university Mr Castel had written him to explain that there would be no more money.

He'd not had any contact from his adopted parents since moving to university when he was eighteen and therefore, he had made Leeds his home. He was surprised that he actually missed them at first, although they were not his real parents and had not shown him any love or affection, they had provided stability and safety, and he had learned valuable life skills from them too. His adopted Mother had taught him domestic skills, she had been a good cook, and he had a real interest in cooking too. His adopted Dad was quite handy, tinkering with cars, gardening and odd maintenance and DIY jobs around the house. He had watched, helped, and picked up those skills too.

He had said that if there was ever a need to visit Edinburgh, he might look them up to see how they are doing. But he doubted very much they would be interested in him.

He also told me that while at university he had allowed friends and friends of friends to store furniture in the empty shops under his flat, all agreed with Rabby of course, and when they didn't return to collect it, Kirk had sold it, accidentally stumbling upon a business opportunity.

He says that he now runs a successful pawn shop in Leeds, providing loans against the value of items, when individuals are unable to get loans from banks. If they are unable to repay the loan the items are then sold. He also buys items at a reduced price when customers need to sell and resells for profit, and he rents the flat above to another university student at a reduced rate to help the girl out financially.

Kirk described himself as independent who liked his own company, he doesn't have many friends and lost contact with school friends and friends from Edinburgh long ago, his university friends have returned to their family homes.

The football lads are not his age, so are not friends either.

He has no girlfriend and lives alone in the house he inherited from his friend Rabby.

He'd played both football and rugby at school and had joined a football academy in

Edinburgh with the ambition of being a professional footballer. That was until the club went into administration ending his chances of a career in football.

He's had several part time jobs, bar work mostly, while at university. He didn't have to of course, Mr Castel, his trustee would send him money whenever he requested it, but he wanted to fend for himself as much as he could, readying himself for the inevitable day that the funding would cease, which it did. He'd manged to save a reasonable amount of money by this time and used his savings as capital for his pawn shop business.

We talked a little about his football team and I'd told him that I didn't know a lot about football, but that my dad was a Leeds United fan.

He'd told me that his football team was from Holbeck, like Leeds United. But unlike Leeds United who's colours are white, yellow, and blue, Holbeck United played in red, white, and black, the colours of bitter rivals across the Pennines, Manchester United.

I learned that Kirk's favourite colour is maroon, after his childhood team, Heart of Midlothian. So, it didn't bother Kirk, that they wore a jersey with red and black halves, and then black shorts and black socks but the lads complained constantly. It wasn't much better when their second kit used to be a white jersey with red trim and any combination of red, white, and black shorts and socks, depending on the colours of the opposition.

The new second kit's all yellow and was the preferred kit of most of the players.

He explained that red, white, and black were the old colours of the club when it was first formed as a railway football team, by railway workers, called Holbeck Railway FC. When the railway yard closed in Holbeck the team almost folded, but instead the club moved its headquarters to The Railway public house in Holbeck and changed the name of the team to Railway FC but didn't change the colours to honour the history of the railway workers club.

Along with many pubs in recent years the business collapsed, and the pub closed its doors, never to reopen, inevitably to be turned in flats.

Holbeck United was then formed retaining the first team colours but change the second kit to all yellow as a nod to the Leeds United team of the 1970s.

The last time Leeds United were any good, Kirk had said, not that either of us were old enough to remember those days. I was born towards the end of the nineties, and I suspected that Kirk was five, or six years my senior.

I had enjoyed our conversation, and hoped that we would have many more, I was not going to let Bex get her hands on him, that was certain, but I could not go over to him now and give him my telephone number, how would that look? I do hope he comes to visit my hotel.

Wrapped in bits of silver.

(Kirk)

What a plum I look like in matching tracksuits with this lot.

I can see the girls from the plane occasionally glancing over, please don't come over I am already getting grief from the lads about you both.

I have got one of your phone numbers, although it's the other one, Lucy, that I would like to see again.

She is tall and elegant, perfectly curvy, with a warm, glowing, reddish-brown skin tone, somewhere between sepia and umber. Her travel outfit choice of a British racing green jump suit and white pumps perfectly complements her look. Hints of copper highlights in her tied up hair sparkly under her sunglasses she is using as a hairband.

Yes, I like her a lot.

I might just have to take her up on her offer and visit that hotel of hers and see if I can find her in the bar or leave a message for her.

Bags collected and team bus waiting, I make a quick escape, a quick stop at our hotel then an afternoon at our training facility.

Cockroach

(Kyle)

I awake a little confused in my hotel room overlooking Dam Square, fuck, I am hanging, rough night, again. I need a little pick me up, a bump.

I have the tester sample in my wallet, which will do, it's too early for a rock star line, so a little pop star line it is.

Mind cleared I'm ready for the tasks ahead.

Now then Mr Harrison, I say to myself, which is the alias I'm currently using. Cash paid for the room meant there was no credit card checks. We have a busy day ahead and anonymity is essential.

I think to myself, if the contact I'm meeting is legitimate, this could get me out of my financial black hole. Black hole? More like an abyss.

I owe money all over Edinburgh, to some very scary people and my wife has let me know under no uncertain terms that the inheritance that she is about to receive is to be invested for the kids and that I will not receive a penny.

We don't know what Mick and Winnie left us in their will yet, but it will be a considerable number, plus the house. A house to which I have never been invited. I would guess £1.5million in total.

I've told her I am away on business for a few days and have asked her to consider an offer. If she gives me £50,000, I will sign everything over to her.

She's agreed to my proposal in principle and is seeking legal advice, Mr Farquarson, her father's solicitor will do anything to ensure I don't receive any of his inheritance money.

She is worth more to me dead.

I would get everything if she were to meet her demise, death in service payment from her fancy job, her pension, her life insurance, our house, her inheritance, and her parents' house too.

I would kill her, I would, but do you know what? Officer Dibble would be knocking on my door first, far too obvious. Motive and opportunity.

It's no secret that our marriage is a disaster. She met the wrong guy.

I need a drink while I await the call from my contact, I can't go to the bar from last night, I will not be welcome there, I will never be welcome there. But what an awesome night it was.

I go to freshen up in front of the hotel bathroom mirror. As I look at my reflection my image starts to buffer and I see a dual image of myself, one of me in pain and the other is of my soul being sucked out of my body. I am paralysed and unable to move, sweat starts to form on my brow and then pour down my face.

What a strange feeling, it felt like someone was walking over my grave as my body shuddered. It was such an eerie experience, did a ghost just enter my body and then leave?

I flop onto the bathroom toilet seat, and I'm exhausted and shaking, I look down at my hands and my commands to move them are ignored, it feels like a spirit has taken over my body, but I feel remarkably at ease, there is a familiarity, like a family member is close, a feeling I imagine twins share,

The feelings fade and I am back in the room alone, I check my eyeballs and my heartrate and wonder whether that was a mental episode, some anxiety regarding today's activities, or was it a combination of the hangover and the cocaine for breakfast?

I decide it's that latter, but the feeling that someone who is familiar to me is remarkably close does not leave my thoughts.

Now, snap out of it, I say to myself, where did they say the meet was to take place? The Cockroach? No, the Grasshopper, a big illuminated green building near the train station.

Short Arms

(Kirk)

The training session was uneventful, gentle impact, mainly stretches and a 13-minute power run.

I did have a funny turn in the locker room after training, through the mist of the hot showers I saw an image of myself waving me over. I tried to wave back but did not have the control of my body.

Did I imagine the figure mouth, 'come with me brother'?

As the figure closed in on me it faded to nothing as it passed through me, I had a strange feeling that the ghosty figure had taken something from me and left something behind within me.

I'd never known my biological family, there is a chance that I have siblings, I had wondered many times about the possibility. Was this a message from a brother, a twin brother?

I had an intense intuition that someone significant was close by.

"Scottish, you look like you've seen a ghost" said Geoff as he collected my kit.

"He's thinking about those birds on the plane" said one of the lads, and a chorus of juvenile whooping and whistling followed.

The nonsense was broken up by Jock announcing that the gaffer has given us the evening off to let our hair down a bit with a midnight curfew. He's suggested that we all go to the Grasshopper pub for 11:30pm, he will get the last drinks in, a nightcap on the gaffer, and we will all walk back to the hotel together. A plan to manage the curfew, a very clever plan to ensure compliance.

We have a 16-man squad for this trip and a friendly with Ajax FC under 21s in 2 days' time. The gaffer, his assistant coach, Jock, Geoff the kit man and Pat, short for Patricia our team medic and physio make up the remainder of the travel party.

Pat wouldn't be concerned about being the only female in the group, she is Jock's wife, and they are a formidable duo.

The Chairman and his wife, Mr and Mrs Short were to be flying out for the match only. The lads guessed that they would be in the city longer than they are letting on, but they certainly will not be staying at Hotel Jimmy.

The Chairman is not so fondly referred to as long-pockets, a saying I learned in Leeds. Short arms and long pockets, referring to a tight sod.

We had paid for our own flights and 50% towards our digs, the remaining costs were being paid for from club funds raised during the season from the club bar, charity events and subs.

The Chairman's short arms had not managed to reach into his long pockets to contribute for this one.

He will be in the executive suite at the Johan Cruyff arena though, quaffing champagne and the rest.

Geoff makes his excuses and leaves to get the training kit ready for the following day.

The gaffer and Jock, have a trip to the arena to look at the facilities, of course they are, and Pat has an evening of viewing art and architecture planned, which she declares is beyond the comprehension of us lager louts. She is not wrong.

I need to exit too, I have an appointment that I cannot miss, the real reason I have travelled to Amsterdam.

Getting away will not be easy though on a team bonding trip, nothing divides a team quicker than a lightweight bailing early on a night on the drinks. I'll stay with the lads until we have the first casualty of the evening, one of them is bound to overdo it, show off and end up either passed out or throwing up, I'll offer to take him back to the hotel, I'll win some valuable team kudos for that gesture.

The lads have voted to skip the evening team meal in favour of heading off into Amsterdam centre. Beers on an empty stomach, what can go wrong? Most of them will be in their beds by 10pm. I need one of them to retire a little before that if I am going to make my business appointment.

ETA

(Kyle)

Finally contact, a text

> *Train delayed. ETA 23:20*

Then a second text from a different number

> *Grasshopper 23:30 DO NOT be late.*

I replied to both message with an 'okay,' but I suspect that they were using a burner phone and doubted that they would have received my message before the sim card had been removed, destroyed, and discarded.

The cocaine deal was happening.

Defenders code.

(Kirk)

And one bites the dust, the new right back who's made the step up from the under nineteens, lays hunched in the corner of the Bulldog bar.

This is perfect, one of my defenders, the defenders code makes this the responsibility of the centre back, me. I step in, faux give the lads a bollocking for being daft and picking on one of my defenders. Just validating why, I am the one to take him back to the hotel.

I get some jeers and heckling from one or two of the lads, but no-one challenges me taking him back.

"Take it easy, Scottish" one of them says.

Not a very imaginative nickname, but milder than most of the nicknames the lads had been given. To be honest most of the lads just call me Kirk, I don't mind either way.

I just might pull this off tonight. It will be tight getting back to the Grasshopper by 11:30pm, but I do like a bit of pressure.

The first casualty of the night put to bed; the hotel receptionist has agreed to check on him every 20 minutes to make sure he is ok.

A quick google search has identified my destination and I have route planned.

Muppet Show

(Kirk)

As expected, my knock on the big black door under the neon sign that read Club Deluxe, was answered by a couple of impressive intimidating security staff.

"Not see the fucking doorbell" one said, in what appears to an eastern European, could be Russian accent.

I had seen the bell, but only after I'd already knocked, there didn't seem much point pressing the bell once I'd already knocked. I just smiled politely.

A petite, good looking women in business attire, peered around the door.

"Fuck off inside you two muppets" she said with a cheeky smile. They both smiled back.

I detected an English accent, quite a posh English accent.

"Yes, boss lady" they both chimed.

"Please Ignore Bert and Ernie" she advised, and I laughed a little too loudly.

"They're both lovely guys really, for trained killers anyway" she whispered.

I didn't laugh this time.

"You must be TenderloinXXL said the English rose.

"I'm Rosie" offering her hand.

No fucking way I thought, an English rose called Rosie, what are the chances?

"Follow me" she commanded.

We stopped outside an impressive wooden door with number 16 displayed in chrome.

"In there you will find a shower and towels, please use them, and make yourself comfortable. Your guest will be joining you shortly" Rosie says in a very matter of fact, business like way.

"Our Russian friends here" she says nodding to Bert and Ernie

"They'll ensure that you're not disturbed, and when you are ready to leave, they'll arrange for my car to take you anywhere you wish to go afterwards. I assume the airport?" Rosie enquires.

I didn't disclose my plans I just said thank you and entered the room.

"Oh, I almost forgot" Rosie says holding my arm.

"Please sign the NDA first, be a good boy" and she points to a document on a table in the room.

I had been expecting to sign a nondisclosure agreement but hadn't questioned why it had not been mentioned sooner.

Document signed and handed to Rosie; I began to remove my shirt.

"My, my, you are a fine specimen" she said.

"No wonder you are in such high demand" Rosie commented in in softer, if not playful tone.

"Will you be in Amsterdam again soon, or maybe I can visit you. Where is home for you Mr Tenderloin" she asked?

"I'm not sure I will be back in Amsterdam anytime soon, but if I am I know which door to knock on" I replied.

And with that she exited the room with a wink.

American Dollars

(Kirk)

The room had all the luxurious splendour of a 5-star hotel, except this room didn't have any windows.

I shaved, took a shower, and dried off most of the excess water from my body, wrapped the towel around my waist and entered the bedroom.

"Hello"

There she was, laid on the bed in a sheer black negligee as if she were resting on a chaise longue. I recognised her immediately, a celebrity, an actress.

"Drop the robe, I want to see what my American Dollars are paying for," said the American actress.

The Myth

(American Actress)

So, there he was, the myth, right in front of me, if I'd reached out, I could have touched it. I wanted to hold it, to gauge how far my petite hand could wrap around it, to feel the heat of it and the weight. But, not so fast, there is plenty of time for that, no need to look too eager I remind myself.

I hadn't believed all the rumours concerning the legend of a British man known as TenderloinXXL. People tend to exaggerate, in my measured opinion, however, not on this occasion it would seem.

Now, to find out if his hands were like magic and what about the stamina, he is fabled for?

"I will start by taking a massage" I said.

English Prick

(Kirk)

Good to Rosie's word I was now in a blacked out stretch limousine.

"Central Station" I told them was my destination.

Rosie's bodyguards, security guards, had thought that I was heading to the airport.

"I don't like to fly" I lied "it's the railway or boats for me."

"Very much like Denis Bergkamp" said Bert, or was it, Ernie.

"The same" I said.

I recalled that the Dutch footballer has a phobia about flying and would miss many European away matches for his club Arsenal because he'd refused to fly.

"I can swim a bit, but I cannot fly at all, I think that was his quote" I added.

"Close enough for me Englishman" Ernie this time, and he gave me an approving pat on the back, which almost knocked the wind out of me.

"I thought English are pricks," said Bert.

"I'm Scottish"

"Explains it then, English still pricks, the world remains balanced" laughs Ernie.

Bert hands me a business card and turns to Ernie to says, "I hope we don't have to kill him."

Bert and Ernie turned to walk back into the big black door after seeing me into the limo.

Shit, I'm not going to get to the Grasshopper in time to meet up with the gaffer and the lads for that last drink, nightcap.

Plan B, I will go straight to Hotel Jimmy and sit with a very pissed right back, I think fifty euros should be sufficient to have the receptionist say that I have been there with him all night.

Thinking on my feet.

'Ping' my HSBC app tells me I have received £2,000. Reference – bodywork

'Ping' another £500 reference - expenses/tip.

I look at the business card Bert handed to me.

Rosie Sparx

r.sparx@fixer.c.uk

+44 7912 755928

If demand slows, contact me. Rx

Pussy Galore

(American Actress)

"Julia, I did it" I declare into the telephone.

"It was everything you said it would be and more."

"The Englishman was incredible, not like our clueless American men."

"Scotsman, darling" says Julia.

"Is there a difference, Julia? Ok, our man from the UK, I feel like a Bond girl" I giggle into the telephone.

"A Bond girl that needs to visit her surgeon for some repair work" I add for dramatic affect.

We both laugh.

'Click.'

Telephone conversation concluded, I say to myself, there is much to do. I need to thank

Rosie "the fixer" for her outstanding hospitality and discretion, and to schedule another appointment.

Then to my private jet.

Will I tell Grant? Yes, yes, I will, my husband has never been the jealous type, we have parties, and he never objects to the things I get up to at our special parties.

We should have another party and fly in my Mr Bond, wouldn't that be neat?

Beast

(Kyle)

I have an hour or so to kill in the red-light district. There is something for everyone, I am not looking for anything specific, just need to scratch an itch. Lose the nervous tension before the meet.

I've been recommended to the businessmen though my contacts in Edinburgh. First time job that could lead to regular transactions. A simple job, just sussing me out.

I'm to collect a bag of money, take it to the meeting at the Grasshopper in exchange for a quantity of cocaine and then return to the location where I collected the money and deliver it there. Simples.

I stop at one of the red illuminated doorways, she looks nice enough.

We agree a price for a thirty-minute session, and I enter. I'm advised that I'm permitted to cum twice in an hour-long booking, I said I would think about it, but thirty minutes is fine for now. I smile to myself; I was in my teens the last time I could recover to go again in the same hour. The door and the curtain are closed across the entrance, indicating the occupants are engaged within.

The room is small, same as them all, there's a toilet and shower in the corner and a bed in the adjacent corner. She's wearing a 2-piece swimsuit in the doorway, by the time I have reached the bed she is completely naked and requests payment up front.

While she takes the money to a safe place I undress and lay on the bed and wait for her return.

Oral without a condom is what she'd offered during negotiations, why would anyone opt for a blow job while wearing a condom? Seems unlikely anyone would, then again, I wonder if it's something the girls insist upon if the customer is not hygienic.

She set about the task vigorously, with extraordinarily little skill. I wondered if she was new to this game but doubted it.

It was obvious that she planned to make me finish as soon as possible, of course this was the objective, who cums twice, really? She's been paid for the thirty minutes, so if I am out of there in 5, she's back on her stool in the doorway waving in the next punter.

I pushed her away "no, rush hen."

I lift her easily and place her onto her tiny bed, sliding my mouth down her body, stopping briefly at the small but pert boobs, on my way to give her the tongue pleasuring of her life. I'll show her how to give oral.

I'm good with my tongue, have a measured technique, starting slowly and gently and then build up the momentum and pressure. She'll soon start to move her hips involuntarily and surrender into a mind-blowing orgasm at the hands of the tongue master.

I look up to observe the pleasure on her face. What the fuck, she is staring at the ceiling and is picking debris from her fingernails. She could not look any more bored if she tried.

If she's not going to participate one of two things will happen, or both, either I will get tongue cramps, or she will have the cleanest nails in Holland. Enough!

I am on top of her in a flash, she realises too late, her staring into space has caught her off guard, I am inside her, she tries to protest but I hold my had over her nose and mouth, so no sound peeps out. She tries to pull away, but I have my weight on her and she is pinned to the bed.

I am too big for her to fight me off and with every deep and heavy thrust she fights a little less, until she is fighting no more.

This is more like it, on my terms, you're not bored now are you lady. I feel powerful, I might just muster the ability to go a second time, and with that I come deep inside her.

As I release my hand from her mouth, I realise that she is unconscious, still breathing but unconscious.

I dress quickly and I am about to leave but then realise that I've left a lot of evidence, I'm smarter than this. I search for cleaning products, there are a lot of wipes and disinfectant sprays. There is also a large box of sex toys, restraints, dildos and various masks and gags.

Hello, I feel another erection, looks like I'm going to get my money's worth after all, and I undress again.

She awakens naturally but is a little confused as she comes around. She is tied and gagged, still naked but has been showered and cleaned.

Face down on the bed, her hands and feet are tied to each corner of the bed, spreadeagled. Ball gag muffling her cries as she tries to look over her shoulders to make eye contact.

I am wearing a mask, not to shield my identity, she has already seen my face. The mask is part of my new character, my alter ego. I am going to have some fun.

I squirt lube on and inside her bum and begin to use my fingers to push the lube deeper and to stretch her. She tries to resist but is bound too tightly, as I climb off her to reach for one of her sex toys her eyes close as she realises the inevitability and her head slumps into the bed in surrender.

If she could scream, she would, as I stand holding her own heavy-duty dildo, in the shape of an arm and a fist, that she no doubt uses on some of her kinky clients. It's her turn to feel it.

Her eyes open and open widely, heavy breathing and snorting from her nose, as she feels the pain of the dildo thrust violently into her, her body tries to contort and her head flails from side to side.

Dildo removed, I lay on top of her once more and whisper in her ear "that will teach you to clean your nails, bitch" and I ram my erection where the rubber fist had just been.

Buffering

(Kirk)

As we approach the station drop off point, I spot the bright green façade of the Grasshopper, where I'm supposed to be rejoining the lads, and I slide down the seat in the back of the limo to avoid being seen.

"Blacked out windows" says a voice from the front seat. Another Russian I believe.

Here it comes again, that funny feeling I had in the shower earlier today. My arms and hands are paralysed, what is happening to me, I have an awful feeling that something awful has happened, have I ingested something. Am I hallucinating, I see blood on my hands and my hands tightening around someone's neck. I glance at the window and see three images of my own face staring back at me buffering. The face in the middle riddled with fear, the images to the right and to the left display a face of pure evil, then the three faces become one and vanish. I look back at my hands and have full mobility back and there is no blood.

"You ok back there" says the driver "You look like shit."

"I'm fine, I think I've eaten something that disagrees with me" I reply. It's a lie, I feel horrendous, and I cannot shake the feeling that something has happened and that someone close to me has hurt someone, badly.

Drug Pilot

(Pat)

On my architectural escapade I had seen the De Gooyer Windmill, The Royal Palace, Central Station. The Portuguese Synagogue, the beautiful catholic church De Krijtberg – Saint Franciscus Xaveriuskerk, The Waag, Café Papeneiland and Café Hoppe and I was uplifted. I had seen the bullet marks on walls left during World War II and it made me sad.

I thought about what life would have been like during that dark days of the war, beautiful buildings occupied by German soldiers, without appreciating their splendour.

I had browsed around the art of Rijksmuseums, Moco and Stedelijk and finally the Van Gogh Museum and discovered the life of Vincent Van Gogh and marvelled at his masterpieces.

The art and architecture of Amsterdam was exhilarating, and exactly why I came to this city of sin. Speaking of sin, I am curious to see what the red-light district is all about.

I find it shocking, but fascinating, titillating. I overhear a group discussing the florescent colours, red for heterosexuals, the ladies in the red illuminated doors are strangely alluring. There is a gay street too I hear, Reguliersdwarsstraat, and blue light illuminated doorways, for both gay men and women.

I had a brief encounter with a girl on a night out while at college, nothing heavy just some soft petting, but I have always wondered whether I would have taken things a little further given the opportunity.

I would not describe myself as bisexual or even bicurious, but I do think women are more physically attractive than men, and I'm attracted to women. It wouldn't be wrong just have look I tell myself.

Wait was that Scottish coming out of that prostitute's doorway.

I only got a glance, but it looked a lot like him, was he wearing fancy dress? I don't recall the lads saying it was a fancy-dress night.

And what was he supposed to be dressed as. He looked half drug dealer and half fighter pilot.

Damn, I have lost him, he made a hasty getaway.

The blue-light district will have to wait for another night.

Big Fish

(Kyle)

The bag of cash was where they said it would be, a locker in the train station with a combination code. Part one complete, no turning back now.

Not that there was any intention of backing out, I need this job to go well. I need the money badly and I need to start swimming with the bigger fish. Small deals in and around Edinburgh were drawing unwanted attention to me. Too much risk for too little gain.

Plus, my reputation for dealing was making me a liability on the doors. Big Dunk, a fellow doorman and school friend of my wife, Isla, had stuck by me and when the Head of Security, Jimmy, had wanted to finish me it was Big Dunk who saved my job and took responsibility for me.

Dunk had pulled me to one side immediately after and said, "I did that for Isla and the kids, don't think about letting me down."

That is why deals away from my homeland are my new business, imports, and exports.

But first to make a good impression with my new associates, that I have yet to meet face to face.

A pint of Guinness in my hand, tucked away in the corner of the Grasshopper, away enough so to not attract attention, I have an unobstructed view of the front door and close enough to the other exit if things go bad.

I have no remorse of guilt for the girl, she will be found eventually. Occupational hazard I tell myself. I left no evidence, and I am in disguise. One small task to complete then I will be out of this outrageous outfit.

If she would just have participated, joined in a little and faked enjoying it, it would have been acceptable. I was surprised that I'd lost his cool so quickly, but when it escalated, I needed to take drastic action to teach her a lesson, and drastic action he had taken.

Yes, when action was needed, I'd reacted swiftly and decisively.

I'd neutralised the chance of her reporting it before completing my business and would be out of Amsterdam before the alarm was raised. The restraints and gag would serve their purpose until she's found, by a cleaner I guessed.

I had done a rather good clean up job myself.

I don't make mistakes; I do not get caught. I know what the police will look for, not that I am concerned that she will report it to the police, my guess is she will not.

I have taken back my one hundred Euros, and all the notes in her drawer, to ensure the money cannot be traced back to me.

Always thinking on my feet.

Drop the Pilot

(Adrianus)

I don't usually do this, I'm not a foot soldier, but I want to see this guy for myself, the guy known as Apparition. Let's see if he really is a ghost.

That must be him in the corner, hugging a Guinness. What does he look like?

Mirrored aviator sunglasses.

Brown pilot jacket with Top Gun style fur collar.

Black rollneck sweater with a thick fake gold chain round his neck.

And how many sovereign rings?

He might as well have petty criminal tattooed on his forehead. If he walks out of here with a holdall he will be pinched before he reaches the bottom step, not that I have brought the holdall. This contact is for me to eyeball the Apparition and decide if I will do business with him. The holdall is safely with my trusted partner.

I don't see the bag with my 20,000 Euros either.

This feels bad. Worse, there is a group of a dozen or so English lads pissed as arseholes attracting far too much attention for my liking.

Dressed like a Count?

(Kyle)

Is there anything worse than drunk English twats?

At least they can't see me tucked away in this corner. I have one eye on them and the other on the bag of money I have secreted between a chair and the wall close enough that if someone spots it that I can claim it, and far enough away that I can disown it if the deal goes bad.

I've just seen a guy walk in, scan the place and leave. It could be my guy, but he didn't look like the type of guy I was expecting, too official looking.

If it was him, what did he see that sent him away?

'ping' text alert

Grasshopper too jumpy for me

'ping' text alert from a different number

> *Free for that coffee if you are, find a nice café and I will find you.*

I'm out of my seat in a flash, heading for my bag. Oh crap, the English lads are heading my way, I put my collar up, and my head down. I brush passed them unnoticed and grab my bag and am almost out of the door.

"Oi, Scottish, is that you? Why are you dressed like a cunt?" I hear one shout.

Did I pause too long, I did not look back, has someone recognised me?

No time to find out, and I'm out in the street, it's busy with cars and people, the dark night sky and the bright lights of buildings and signs contradict each other, confusing me momentarily. I cross a street, and down another street, I can see it's called Damrax and disappear into the first café I find, Café Van Beeren.

I have not looked back since I left the Grasshopper, was I followed? I order a beer and take the opportunity to scan the streets around the café, people are moving idly by. Drunken couples' arm in arm heading home after a too many beers, a middle-aged guy unsteady on his feet, swaying from side to side and bumping into obstacles, but I can't see anyone following me or watching the Café.

'ping' text alert

> *Lose the jacket, shades, and imitation jewellery.*

That was the message I was waiting for that would signal that the coast was clear for the deal,

'ping'

> *Insomnia Coffee Shop, 10 mins*

Milkshake Boys

(Kyle)

A quick toilet visit, disguise dumped in a bin, and I'm out of Café Van Beeren and into the night of Amsterdam once more. I have slipped out of the back exit just to make sure that I'm not followed.

The streets are as active as they've been all night and I'm wondering if anyone sleeps in this city as I arrive at the aptly named Insomnia Coffee Shop.

The coffee shop is lively, the music is louder than I would have expected, although the customers continue their conversations regardless.

I see the man I spotted earlier at the Grasshopper sat at the bar at the very rear of the coffee shop.

As I approach and before I have the chance to speak, he says.

"Have a milkshake" I am guessing he's Dutch.

"Not for me" I reply.

"Have a fucking milkshake" he snaps.

"Pieter makes fucking good milkshakes, best in the world" he says, in a little more friendly tone.

"He will roll you a blunt too if that's your thing" he adds.

"That would be most pleasant" I say, thinking I have not heard a joint being called a blunt for a long time.

"Pleasant, you hear that Pieter?" he laughs.

"Either he's trying to impress you boss, or he's one of those posh English lords" says Pieter, in a very distinct Dutch accent.

"He did not look like an English gent, earlier Pieter, now did he? More, what did you say, Naval Aviator" says the boss?

And they both burst out singing 'you've lost that loving feeling' and share a little laugh.

A few of the young customers, stoned, glance over. Pieter squirts water at them from the soda handgun.

"Mind yours" he says, and they return to their smoking.

"I'm Scottish" I say but the moment has passed.

"The name is Keitel, Mr Harvel Keitel" the boss says shooting out his hand.

"Pleasure to meet you" says Mr Keitel

Pieter starts to laugh and to shake his head "Fuck boss."

"OK, Pieter has given the game away, I am not Mr White."

A Reservoir Dogs reference I understand.

"But you can call me Harvey anyway, I don't believe in using real names, so I am Harvey, you will be called Irish" says Harvey.

"I'm Scottish" I say again.

"I am being ironic, Irish it is, settled" says Harvey.

"Now Irish" Harvey says in low and serious voice.

"Hand that bag over to Pieter, he doesn't count it, he will guess from the weight if the money is correct."

"Really" I say.

"No, Irish, you really are a gullible twat, give him the money" laughs Harvey.

"Here's our bag in return, I trust that you don't need to check that either?" says Pieter.

"Now disappear" says Harvey.

"And do not go back to Café Van Beeren to pick up your fancy dress outfit" Harvey orders as he turns back to his milkshake at the bar.

They have been watching me, of course they have, 'that loving feeling' reverberating behind me as I leave the Insomnia.

All part of the service
(Kirk)

"Role call" shouts the Gaffer.

I can hear the discussion in the reception area from my room.

"Two of your party have been here since 9:30ish" says the receptionist.

"A tall drink of water on a hot day, not unpleasing on the eye, and a young boy that was sick from alcohol I guess" she continues.

"Ok, what about, Geoff and Pat" askes the Gaffer

"I'm right behind you" says Pat "you say Kirk has been here all night" Pat enquires to the receptionist.

"All night" replies the receptionist "I looked in on them every 20 minutes, just to make sure the boy was not sick, it's an extra charge at Hotel Jimmy if guests throw up".

Clever reply I thought, if she'd not explained why she was checking on us every 20 minutes, it wouldn't be believable, the financial penalty clause gave it gravitas.

"Kirk is a good man" say Pat "and thank you for looking in on them."

"All part of the service here at Hotel Jimmy" says the receptionist and the disappears into her office behind the desk.

"Where's Geoff" asks Jock.

"Sleeping on the bus, I'd guess" says Pat to her husband. "Let's leave him there, Jock, he'll sleep a while then he'll be up checking the training kit and equipment again."

"Breakfast 8 am sharp" shouts the Gaffer, and the hotel falls silent, save for the odd burp, fart, and occasional giggling.

I go past Jock and Pat's room and surprisingly the door is open. What's happening here, I think to myself.

"Hi Kirk" says Pat who is now behind me in the hotel kitchen "Can't you sleep."

"I've had a few hours already while babysitting, just getting some water, You?" I reply.

"How is he" She asks.

"He'll be fine, he'll be rough in the morning, but he's young enough to run it off in training tomorrow" I say.

"Didn't you fancy leaving him here and meeting up with the lads again" Pat enquires.

"That was my absolute intention, Pat, but the lady on reception made it clear that it was my responsibility to stop him throwing up, and if he did throw up, there'd be a big bill to pay. Do you know what, Pat? she checked every 15 minutes or so" I said, Confirming the receptionists story.

"That is incredibly good of you to do that, Kirk, the team need someone with maturity to take responsibility. The Gaffer will be pleased with you" Pat adds.

"That might be so, but I was just looking out for the kid."

"Night, Kirk"

"Night, Pat"

Swelling

(Pat)

So, it wasn't Kirk that I saw coming out of the doorway in the red-light district.

I wouldn't judge him if it had been him, he is a single guy, it's just that I wouldn't have thought he would need to get his satisfaction that way. I know that's hypocritical since I was going to visit the blue-light district, I was kidding myself that I just wanted to have a harmless look, but the reality is I yearned for touching another woman's body, especially breasts. I like big boobs.

Touching another woman, massaging another woman's breasts isn't cheating, is it? A little kissing. Definitely not cheating, just harmless fun I agree with myself.

Anyway, it wasn't him, he can't have been in two places at once, his story checks out, corroborated by the receptionist. Too neatly for my liking, she certainly liked our big Scottish centre back, didn't she? What did she call him? 'A long drink of water on a hot day,' that was it.

Whenever we go away as a team, he always has the ladies watching him, and more, asking after his story, is he single. Is he available?

He's not arrogant about it either, which just makes him more attractive as far as I'm concerned, he's a remarkable man. I do hope it wasn't him in the pilot outfit.

And that body, wow, as the physio and medic I have had my hands on parts of his body those ladies fantasise about.

I've had fantasies too; I am only human after all. I love Jock, I always have and always will, he is one of life's good guys and I am a better person with him. We are a good couple together, a happy couple I think to myself.

My mind wanders through to the ball in the groin incident.

We were 2-1 up, against local rivals, and they had a free kick just outside the area, with only a few minutes to go in the match. Kirk was in the defensive wall, to give the wall height, and he was frantically trying to organise the left back to mark their right winger, who was making a late run into the box. Kirk was pointing at the runner with the hand that should have been protecting the crown jewels, when their player takes a quick free kick and the ball flies, at pace, into Kirk's groin. Everyone on the pitch groaned with him, everyone on the sidelines turned away.

I arrived at the scene, and I had to push my way past both teams who had surrounded him to see if he was ok, he was not ok, he was rolling around on the ground. As I knelt next to him, stupidly asking where it hurts, he pulls his shorts down and starts cupping his own balls for comfort.

I say, "you'll have to come off, Kirk, there's severe swelling to your penis."

"No Pat, that is it's normal size" he says, and the lads all start to laugh.

I blushed and tried to hide my face from the laughing crowd, hurriedly put my medical gear away and made a hasty run for the touch line. Despite my embarrassment I was thinking to myself, that is anything but normal size Kirk. I have never seen anything like it, I have never heard of anything like it. Ridiculously, freakishly huge!

Breadcrumbs

(Kyle)

I had the cocaine in my possession for only a matter of hours, delivering it safely to the Intercontinental Hotel, Royal suite, where I collected my 5,000 Euro commission fee and had been provided with train tickets and fake travel documents back to Edinburgh, via Paris and London.

I guessed they were Russian, but it was none of my business, it was easy money, easy money that I desperately needed. I had played the part well, I thought. A youngish, up and coming distributor known as "The Apparition" who would take all the risks, anonymously, moving money and product from gang to gang, family to family, without their family members and gang members being associated with the deals, if it went south. If the deal did go bad, I would take fall, the others would not be implicated and this was my USP, my Unique Selling Point.

As far as my new associates were concerned, this was the start of something big, if it worked out of course. I had other ideas.

I'd my passport checked twice already, I'd slept a bit, so had left my papers open for the boarding checks to be conducted without me being disturbed, plus I didn't want to be seen.

My ticket and passport were in order, and I was left to sleep in my first-class seat, I did wonder whether a more thorough check would have been taken if I were in standard accommodation.

What was it that one of those security guards said at the Intercontinental? What had he called me? I'd paid no attention at the time, but it keeps bugging me.

'Look here, it's the Scottish Denis Bergkamp again,' one had said to the other and they both laughed.

That was weird I thought. And brushed it off.

Then it was back, stopping my sleep, how did they know I was Scottish? I hadn't spoken. I definitely didn't speak; I handed over a bag and picked up a bag and that was it.

Mr White and his bartender, Pieter, knew I was Scottish, that must be it, but why would they communicate with the other family. The idea was that there didn't have to be any contact between them. That just didn't make any sense, it's the minute details that get you caught in this game, I need to know what this is all about, but how.

Who is Denis Bergkamp?

Ask Google, Denis Bergkamp, age 55, former footballer now coach. Played for Arsenal and Inter Milan, seems he was a rather talented and successful footballer. Phobia about flying. Was that the joke between the two security guards. Of course it was, they knew I was traveling to Edinburgh and by train, they assumed I don't like to fly, which is true.

That is, that, I can have some shut eye now.

'Again.' They said 'Again.'

'Look here, it's the Scottish Denis Bergkamp, again.'

Where had they seen me before?

Anyway, I'm now far away from Holland, travelling home at high speed for an ultimatum. Just a small detour first, two birds, one stone I thought.

'ping'

> *I do hope that you are far, far away from Amsterdam Mr Apparition, what a terrible mess you have left behind in the red-light district.*
>
> *There are some extremely dangerous men looking for an Irishman that looks like Biggles.*

They have found your clothes in a bin in Café Van Beeren, some receipts in the pockets give away your identity, is the information I have received.

Disappear is my advice, we do not know each other, and we have never met. Understand?

H

A warning from 'H', Harvey K, AKA Mr White from the Insomnia Café, or Adrianus as he's known. He wasn't fooling me with his Reservoir Dogs nonsense in front of his barman. I knew your identity all along Mr Adrianus Bakker, and you know it.

So, she didn't go to the Police, I didn't think she would. But her bosses are a different story, she would have had to tell them that she had no earnings to hand over and explain that she would be out of action for a while.

My plan has worked, the disguise deliberately absurd, as deliberate as the receipts left in the pockets, let's call it insurance. What will they find exactly? a receipt for a Guinness at the Grasshopper, another for a beer at Café Van Beeren, where did I go next Milkshake man? Ah, yes, I am sending them straight to you.

Thinking on my feet, always.

I am disappeared now anyway, travelling under a different name and with a new disguise.

Voodoo

(Rosie)

I've received a notification that I have an encrypted email via the dark web. This is the recognised and acceptable way to contact me, "The Fixer".

The message is from the call sign, Voodoo, who I know to be Vander. Vander runs prostitution in Amsterdam, owns most of the property in the red-light district, therefore controlling the windows. He also engages in a bit of human trafficking.

It's true that prostitution is legal in Amsterdam, and many of the workers are registered and have certificates and permits, they also have health insurance and pay their taxes just like any independent worker.

The Police and local council control and monitor activity to prevent exploitation of minors and undocumented immigrants, but the controls are not robust enough to prevent Vander making an extremely lucrative business.

His email is direct, it usually is.

> Problem, to solve, usual covert contact desired.

I can guess both the problem and the solution he requires, but I will call him anyway on an encrypted video call.

His problem – one of his girls has been violently assaulted.

The solution – find who did it.

"Good morning, Voodoo" I say as his image appears.

"Electra" He replies, which is my call sign on this service, a play on Sparx.

"You have a problem for me to help you with?" I ask.

"I do" says Voodoo.

He goes on to explain some basic details, very matter of fact as if he's reporting a defect to kitchen appliance.

Girl found bound and gagged in the early hours, assaulted. Physically and psychologically damaged. Assailant was in fancy dress; reports suggest Top Gun Pilot.

Police not involved, nor will they be.

What is that, fancy dress did he say, Top Gun Pilot? This is new information I did not know before the call; however, this information is gold dust, because I know this person I say to myself.

"Any intel, Electra?" he asks.

"Your person of interest is known to my organisation but is not one of my interests" I say "He's known to me through association" I add, he wouldn't have believed that I had no intelligence to share.

"Let me see if I can get my associates to meet with you to share information" I offer.

The call is ended.

I do know that the gentleman in question is known as "The Apparition" and has left Amsterdam by train under the name Mr Arnot McCann. I also know that the same man presented himself as go between for Maksin Volvov and Adrianus Bakker.

Maksin had given Apparition 20,000 Euros to pay for and collect a quantity of high-quality cocaine from an unknown supplier, the supplier is not unknown to me. The supplier is Adrianus.

It would appear to me that Maksin is buying some of his competitions product to assess the quality, while not knowing who he's dealing with. This is unlikely to end well.

I have it on good authority that Maksin had Mr Apparition, and his money followed by one of his men, and that The Apparition was wearing a pilot outfit when he entered the café and ditched it there and exited the back door, losing Maksin's man. The next stop for our protagonist was Insomnia Coffee Shop, an establishment known to both Vander and Adrianus.

Adrianus, is the main player in the import and export of class A drugs in Amsterdam. Every now and then he has to take out a small player who has designs on expansion and a greater market share. Adrianus certainly has the resources to take care of this type of move.

He has no problem with one or two small players on his patch, they generally take the attention away from his business, so they can offer an advantage. The problem arises when they try to expand and affect his business interests.

Occasionally, a major player will make a move to assess the strength of Adrianus Bakker and his family, and a mini war, usually a swift battle ensues that the Bakker family win.

Was Maksin Volvov making a move, time would tell, although taking business by force is not the Volvov way.

There were also strong known links between the Bakker family and Vander's operations, but only because Adrianus permitted it to be so.

Outwardly the Bakker family and in particular Adrianus opposed the human trafficking and exploitation rackets of Vanders business, but Adrianus was receiving a big slice of the financial pie, so Vander was allowed to continue his activities, closely monitored by the Bakker family. Very closely was my intel.

Adrianus is a well-known and respected businessman, who attends many high-profile functions and has many high-profile contacts and friends. Vander's real identity is known only to a select few, Adrianus is one of them and I am another, to everyone else his identity is a mystery.

I was in Maksin's suite when The Apparition arrived to hand over the cocaine, no fancy dress, and he left as Mr Arnot McCann.

Maksin Volvov has an extraordinary business and extensive resources, both financial and in terms of personnel.

He's not a ruthless businessman as one might expect of a Russian gangster family. He's no push over and neither is his family, but the Volvov ethos is to create a network of partners and customers based on mutual respect without fear that establishes their business model.

This business model, is very unlike a Russian gangster but a model the family believe in. However, should the partnership not be mutual respectful, the consequences for those who broke the psychological contract is severe, as severe as the most extreme of gangster families.

He is evaluating Western Europe for expansion, but only if he can find collegial partnerships. It's likely therefore that Maksin's deal using the go between was to open the possibilities to partner with the Bakker family.

Fixing a meeting between the two parties might be beneficial to my organisation too.

My next calls would be to Maksin, call sign Iron-Bear and to Adrianus, AKA, Dusk-Shadow.

A terrible business

(Adrianus)

Pieter said that he'd received a visit at the Coffee Shop, customers had been asked to leave, and he had been interviewed, severely by Maksin's men.

I suspected that it would not be long before Irish and the bag of money was tracked to a meeting with me.

It's not common knowledge that I own the Insomnia Coffee Shop, and I'm rarely seen there, so I am now regretting that I chose that for our final rendezvous with The Apparition, leading our friends to the door.

Pieter confirms that they were not looking for me, just a guy who had left a jacket in Café Van Beeren and had stated loudly down his mobile phone, that he was heading to the Insomnia Coffee Shop. Looks like our Mr

Apparition was leaving a breadcrumb trail to my door.

A meeting was arranged through the fixer and here I am. The meeting is with Vander, people trafficker and pimp I would call him. It doesn't matter to me how a man makes his money, but that's a trade that upsets me. He's powerful and not to be crossed so I keep my feelings to myself. He describes himself somewhat differently. Partnership Consultant is how the peddler of misery presents himself.

We are at a neutral and secret location, our respective bodyguards are watching the entrance and exit, our families respect each other, and we keep our businesses separate, there is no conflict of interest. Until now, my new associate has gone rogue, and I am not sure how to play this situation yet. If I must throw Mr Apparition under a bus I will, but if I can keep our deal quiet I will.

As I enter the private members area, there is a man I don't recognise, a big man, dressed impeccably.

Vander approaches me, hand outstretched.

"Adrianus, let me introduce Maksin."

I've heard of Maksin, of course I have, he's started some import and export of antiques, and a small quantity of drugs, in Amsterdam, nothing to get worked up about, yet. A well-established business in Lithuania and Belarus I understand, and the one he used to have in Ukraine, temporarily suspended.

"This is most irregular Vander" I say,

"This is not how we businessmen operate in Holland. We have our code" I continue.

"With the utmost respect to you gentlemen, I feel a little ambushed" as I take my seat by the fire.

"Not at all Adrianus" Maksin responds before a very sheepish Vander has the opportunity to speak.

"I'm visitor in your fine city, if my business or business associates have left a stain in your city that has an impact on my reputation as a businessman, I must, I am compelled to clean up mess" Maksin bellows, whacking his fist on the table, for dramatic effect.

"There is no ambush, Adrianus, I'm here to apologise and to assist Vander in identifying the rapist" says Maksin in a softer voice as he slumps into the chair opposite me.

"A terrible business" he concludes and lights a cigar.

Maksin offers cigars to Vander and me.

"Now what do we collectively know about the Irishman, we are looking for" Maksin says as he leans forward in the chair resting his arms on his knees.

I like Maksin, I decide, but business is business.

I'm not yet at a stage where I wished to disclose that I had been doing business with the Irishman, if I did, not only would I be implicated in the crime against one of Vander's employees, but this would also expose that Maksin had purchased his drugs from me through our mutual contact.

The reason I'd engaged in the deal with our Mr Apparition, is to look into my opposition business, I had suspected it was Maksin but was not sure.

It was established that the man we were looking for was:

Six foot four or five

He was in fact Scottish not Irish.

Dark brown hair

Good looking

Large, muscular build, rugby player physique or gym body

Not very clever, had been the conclusion of Pieter at the café and the waitress at Café Van Beeren

Loner, not affiliated with another family or gang we agreed.

He's left Amsterdam, Maksin advises, with a supplied forged passport and travel papers, and First-Class rail ticket to Edinburgh under the name of Mr Arnot McCann

I started to make a call to a contact in Edinburgh to pick up Mr McCann when he arrived in the Scottish capital but cut my call short when Maksin received a call that our Mr Apparition, Irish, Mr Arnott Mcann, whatever he was calling himself had vanished.

A contracted hitmen hired by Maksin, was due to board the train at Paris but he'd received a call from his tracker that he had vanished. He had left a pile of clothes, and empty holdall and the passport and train ticket on his First-Class seat.

He knew we were coming for him; he was cleverer than we thought, what if the fool act was just that, playing the fool? The fancy dress, the gullible fool behaviour, all an act.

Genius, very Columbo like, the character played by Peter Falk. Play the fool – to catch a fool.

We had been played.

Was he assessing our businesses, getting inside our businesses, and to what aim?

The 20,000 Euro deal was small fry, a tester for future business, I think both he and I knew that it was unspoken but implied.

I had still not declared my interest in our vanishing man, as far as Vander and Maksin were concerned, I was a respected businessman in Europe, and they were aware of my extensive interests in Amsterdam.

They knew that I would get word of the attack in the city, and I would soon know of the man they were looking for, out of mutual respect between the families I was invited to this parlay.

As for Maksin, he said that he'd been approached be a friend of a friend of a friend, to give this new entrepreneur, The Apparition, a chance to prove himself.

He'd not liked the idea from the start, due to the arrogant name he had afforded himself. Maksin was a movie fan, no particular genre, his taste was diverse. However, he would recoil when characters had ridiculous secret identities or alter egos, Baran Francois Toulour, in Oceans 12, as The Night Fox, Sir Charles Lytton as the Phantom in the Return of the Pink Panther, and Robert De Niro's character Louis Cypher, far too obvious as Lucifer, Satan himself, in the film Angel Heart, although he did like the story of Harry Angel the private Investigator assigned by Louis Cypher to find a musician called Johnny Favourite.

Maksin explains that Angel is actually Johnny Favourite who had made a pact with the devil but had suffered neurological trauma from injuries, had received facial reconstruction and had avoided his deal with the devil. In the end the devil caught up with him, a good film but the Louis Cypher alter ego did not fool him one bit.

He did quite like the Verbal Kint's alter ego, Keyser Zoze, in Usual Suspects though.

The Apparition was almost rejected, but then one of a Maksin's lovely girlfriends had said business is business, and that was that.

So here he was he said, doing a dime deal with an alter ego, with an ego. He had no need to pay 5,000 Euros commission for a 20,000 score of white powder. He had scores of employees who would play runner for a few lines of the cocaine. The aim was to check this Apparition out to see if he could be trusted to move vast quantities.

Maksin had thought he had him where he wanted him, he knew a little bit about him, he knew he hailed from Edinburgh, or that's what his contact had said, he was not so sure now. He had a man, a tracker, who had followed him from the moment he had the bag of money, but who'd lost him at Café Van Beeren, he had the same man on the train following him back to Scotland, but he'd lost him somewhere between Brussels and Paris, probably Lille. He could tolerate one mistake; we were not expecting an outfit change in the Café. But two mistakes in two days, not acceptable, the punishment would be severe. The hitman would have a new target in Paris.

He'd put a tracker in with the money, but the Apparition had left this with the belongings on the train.

He at least now had a description of the man he wanted to talk to.

Maksin offered to compensate Vander as a gesture of goodwill between the families, and to pay for the girl's medical bills, Vander declined politely, he was responsible for the security and safety of his own girls, and he did not hold Maksin responsible.

Vander had said that he would find the man and he would pay, I do not need his money either he had said. He will pay though.

We all vowed to do what we could to search for the Apparition, but we all knew that it was likely that he had vanished, just like a ghost. Plus finding him was not a business priority for any of us, but we agreed that information about his whereabouts would be shared.

Here's looking at you kid.

(Kyle)

There goes that goon again. I recognise him, but from where? I saw him talking with the Ticket Inspector as I boarded the train in Amsterdam, but I swear I had seen him before.

There he was again at Brussels station on the platform, was he scanning passengers getting off or had I imagined it?

Now he is frantically searching the train for something or someone. Now, I have placed him. He was the man that walked past café Van Beeren as I was ordering my beer. He looked like an ordinary tourist then, heading home after a long night stumbling in the dark. It's definitely him though, now looking more alert and industrious. I would wager that he's looking for me and I would guess that he was following me then too, losing me when I slipped out of the back door of the Café after ditching my clothes. I wondered how long he waited before entering the café and how long it took him to discover my disguise in the bin? Presumably, he was the one that discovered my breadcrumb trail of receipts.

How had I missed him in Amsterdam, I was alert to being followed. I'd been careful; I'd taken measures to avoid being tracked. That could have been a disaster I tell myself.

He's perfect for the job though, unremarkable, and forgettable, perfect for tracking people, unnoticed.

I've blended in now nicely with a young lady and her children, I'm asking her for directions but making it appear to onlookers, and the goon, that I belong with this French family.

As the train pulls away from Lille station, next stop Paris, I see the goon discover my pile of clothes and pick up his mobile phone. He's not seen me; I'm sure of that.

I'd anticipated Maksin's next move. I had made it easy for them to follow my departure from Amsterdam, which is why they'd let their guard down. Would they have followed me all the way to Edinburgh? I don't know. But that was never going to happen, not when I'm in the driving seat, my meticulous planning has worked a treat.

Now then Mr Tomas McCloud, Tam, I say to myself. Let us see what Lille has to offer a travelling businessman, tomorrow I'll visit the city and then on to Cherbourg to catch the ferry to Poole.

Set plays.

(Kirk)

That was more like it, the training session was intense. I'm a big unit, and I need to train hard; my fitness regime needs to be regular and high impact cardio for me to stay in shape and maintain my stamina.

I have a fitness instructor back in Leeds that I see once or twice a week, these sessions are reserved for weights to work on strength and muscle sculpting.

In the morning, initially we had a long session of stretches, then a mid-distance run, then a 13-minute sprint. Then we had a lung busting bleep test. Three of the lads threw up, the first to go was the right back. But fair play to him, he was straight back to it and trained solidly all day, overcompensating, but he showed a tremendous heart and mentality.

After a light lunch, and a break, we had some more stretches, then there were a number of small-sided games, focussing on keeping the ball, one and two touches.

We were about to break and split into two groups to practice set piece moves, when we were approached to have an 11 a side session with a local college team. We didn't play a full 90 minutes, but it was intense and as it turned out fantastic preparation.

We played well against an athletic and technically skilful Dutch team. I scored two headed goals from set pieces in a 4-0 win, I'd scored only two goals in the previous season and had felt a little more composed and relaxed today, maybe because I knew this would be the last season at this level.

After the match during the warm down the gaffer had called me over. Here we go I thought, although I knew I had played well I knew he favoured a youthful team, I was expecting to be dropped to the bench for the game at the Johan Cruyff Arena. I was readying myself to take it with dignity I was gutted. I wanted to walk out onto a professional football pitch again, and probably for the last time, look up at the stands, see fans, and soak it all in.

"I heard what you did last night, Son" said the gaffer putting his arm around me and started to walk me away from the lads.

"Oh" I said, here it comes, out of earshot of the team.

"That level of responsibility and leadership is what I'm looking for from you this season, I hear you gave a few of them a flea in their ear."

"Captain Material, that Son"

"I don't know about that" I said, "I was just getting the kid home."

"It wasn't a question, Son."

"You are captain tomorrow and for the rest of the season, it doesn't matter if we get hammered tomorrow, you are captain for the season" and he starts to walk away.

He looks back and says, "Hell of a game you had today."

"Remember, the lads are looking up to you on and off the field for direction and discipline."

I am stunned, what the fuck just happened there.

"Their coach asked about you, asked if you were a ringer, a pro" he laughed.

"The biggest complement I have for you came from Jock, usually he has a word or two to put things in perspective for an outstanding performance, pointing out a mistake or two, out of position he'll say."

Today Jock said just two words, "Fucking Captain."

Lone Wolf

(Rosie)

I'd not been involved in the fixing of The Apparition with either Maksin or Adrianus, but it appeared to me that someone had certainly made it look like it was me.

I did fix the meeting between Vander and Maksin, and I had set up the meeting between Adrianus and Vander, I didn't know however that Maksin was to be there. Not my problem I did as asked, it's on Vander that he allowed Maksin to be present.

I have bigger problems to consider. I had heard the name Apparition but had no means of contact. I understood that he had been a recommendation to Maksin, Maksin was happy to share this detail. Adrianus had not shared how he and the Apparition had met, nor did he surrender the information to either Vander or Maksin that he knew who the

Apparition was, or that he was the other party in the drug deal.

Adrianus was aware that I knew he was the other guy, but he also knew it would stay with me, and he trusted that I was not involved with Maksin.

I'm not involved with anyone; I'm my own boss. I talk about my organisation, but there is no organisation, it is just me, and my two most trusted friends, my Russian bodyguards, and our driver.

On this occasion my reputation was working against me, Maksin assumed I must know the man they seek, because of my substantial contacts and networks.

Bert and Ernie came to my rescue, as usual, big, and daft they may be, but fiercely loyal.

"Boss Lady not involved with dealings of rapist," said Bert.

"That boy a lone wolf" adds Ernie.

"We know what gang member look like, he has no gang, no code" Ernie continues.

Maksin seemed to agree with the assessment of my men.

When Maksin had left, the three of us had agreed that the description was spectacularly close to our Mr Tenderloin.

"Same guy" Bert offers.

"Rapist and Denis of Scotland, be same Guy" Bert adds.

"Although, Vlad, when we called rapist guy 'Scottish Denis Bergkamp, he did not get reference," said Ernie.

"Think he didn't expect to see us at Maksin's hotel, is all" Bert says unconvincingly with a shrug of the shoulders.

I ask the big apes if they think it possible that after Mr T has provided a service to the American actress that he then goes into the city to find a cheap hooker and rapes her?

The boys both agree that it doesn't sound plausible, yet someone looking remarkably like him, identical in fact has turned up to collect drug money and is also wanted for a violent attack.

"How is possible that he in two places at same time" says Bert.

"Twins" says Ernie.

"Doppelganger" I say.

"What is doppelganger" they both ask.

"An apparition or double of a living person, a harbinger of evil" I explain.

"Dr Jekyll and Mr Hyde?" asks Ernie.

"We have problem boss" says Bert.

"Not if we keep this between us, no one will know that there is a chance that our man is the man they seek" I tell them both.

I set out our position to my team.

"Nobody fitting his description visited Club Deluxe."

"No important client was visited."

"There was no Limo drop off."

"Whoever visited the young lady in the red-light district was not our guy."

"Our guy is not that guy."

"Our guy left Amsterdam, before the attack."

We all agreed that we were the only three people that were aware of the possibility of our man's involvement and that common knowledge of that that would be bad for business.

Alter ego, twin or Doppelganger, we would find out.

Me casa su casa

(Kirk)

"Captain?" says Pat as she gives me a post training massage.

I have faked a tight hammy to get out of spending time with the team, I suspect they are going to head into Amsterdam for more drinks, I heard talk of a sex show at a place called Casa Rosso. The lads are doing a whip-round to get one of us up on stage to be one of the acts.

"Aye, it seems that way" I reply.

"The gaffer says I have to sort your joints and muscles out for the game tomorrow, if you don't play as well as you did today it's on me!" says Pat.

"So, I'm going to be thorough" she whispers in my ear.

Oh, crap I think, last time she had her hands on me was the ball in the groin incident. Hope she's not going to check on my swelling.

"Thanks for the heads up, if I play crap, I'll tell him my calves were tight" I retort.

I was going to say groin, but I was concerned that she would concentrate on that area, if she did, there'd be more swelling occurring, involuntarily.

"Hmm" she says, "Does our new captain have a girlfriend yet."

"No comment" I offer.

"Any person of interest" she enquires.

"No bloody comment" is my response "is this a massage or an interrogation?"

"I'm a woman highly skilled at both" she chortles "I have vays of making you talk" she says in a terrible German accent, whilst digging her thumbs into my sciatic nerve for dramatic effect.

"Bloody hell" I cry out "ok I'll talk" I surrender.

"No girlfriend but there's a person of interest as you say that I might pursue" Hoping that that is the end of it, I should have known better.

"The girl on the plane?" is her reply, fishing further.

I don't reply.

"I'll take your silence as confirmation, but which one? I think I would say the one in green, she is incredibly beautiful, Kirk" Pat says.

"She is" is my reply.

"Stays between us" she says "medic-client privilege" she snorts with an overly enthusiastic laugh.

"I'm not sure a part time physio is bound by client privilege" she adds "But it stays with me anyway, me and Jock that is."

"Thanks, she's on the same flight back with us, they're staying at a hotel just down the road from us. I've been invited for drinks at the hotel bar."

"You should go."

"Curfew tonight"

"I'll cover for you; I could advise that you need a 20-minute walk to stretch out your hamstring".

"I don't think so Pat, not a good look for a new captain."

"You're probably right, Kirk."

"Changing the subject completely" says Pat.

"Were you at the Grasshopper at 11:30pm last night, dressed as a Top Gun Fighter Pilot?

"What?" I laugh.

"Some of that lads said they saw you, shouted after you, but you dashed off" She continues the questioning.

"A Fighter Pilot eh, the lads must have stumbled on a stag do. As you know, Pat, I was tucked up in my cot, with a solid alibi. Not that I need one" I laugh.

Now I understand the line of questioning I think to myself, I wasn't spotted getting out of the limousine after all. Pissed up lads thinking they saw someone who looked a little bit like me. I'm not worried about that; my whereabouts have been verified and my secret assignation remains so.

Gotcha

(Pat)

Two sightings of the Fighter Pilot in one night, I thought drug dealer myself, but yes, I can see why the lads thought Top Gun.

It's far too much of a coincidence that Kirk excuses himself from the night out, on the same night that a lookalike is seen both coming out of a prostitute's room in the red-light area of Amsterdam, and at the Grasshopper at the exact time we had agree to meet.

His alibi consists of an unconscious under nineteen football player and an unconvincing receptionist who has eyes, and other body parts, fixated on him.

It's none of my business, but something doesn't sit right with me.

I'd guess that he dressed in fancy dress to disguise himself so he could visit a 'lady of the night' without being seen, but then forgot he was still wearing the ridiculous outfit when he arrived at the Grasshopper. Did he spot himself in a mirror or something and realises his mistake before making a hasty exit?

The holdall, yes, the holdall contains your change of clothes, doesn't it? Gotcha!

Two questions remain, however.

Why would he be visiting prostitutes? and can the prostitute change her mind when she sees what I've seen?

She'd surely be out if action for a while after his visit.

Oh, one final question that has just occurred to me, where's the holdall?

Too many Cook(e)s

(Kirk)

The gaffer tends to surprise us from time to time. He's demanded that we're all back on the coach at 6pm, wearing our team tracksuits, no other kit needed.

It was a relatively brief 30-minute coach ride to the Johan Cruyff Arena, a tour of the football stadium first, a stroll on the perfect playing surface and then to the changing room. Our kits were laid out at individual sections in the most amazing facility I had ever seen or imagined. The team were in absolute silence at first, then euphoria ensued as they saw that we were playing in all yellow and they saw their names on the backs of the shirts.

The team sheet and formation were displayed on the wall on flipchart sized paper, a white board with football pitch markings and yellow and red magnets, denoting players, for the coaching staff to demonstrate tactics, was in the centre of the locker room.

1 Wilcock

6 Thomas   16 McDonnel(C)

2 Glover   3 Donachie

4 Hunter

7 Robson   8 Graham   11 Ali

10 Cooke. D

9 Hussain

Subs.

5 Bow, 12 Cook, 13 Chang, 14 Singh,15 Cooke. S,

There I was, number 16, McDonnel, with the captain's armband pinned to the left sleeve.

As we sat in our individual booths, the gaffer made three comments.

One, these kits were commemorative. The jerseys were for us to keep, in the centre of the shirt in-between the sports brand logo and the club badge, embroidered in black on the yellow background it displayed:

AFC Ajax U21

V

Holbeck United

19th July

Long pockets had dug deep, and we were impressed.

Two, Kirk McDonnel, was club captain tomorrow and for the rest of the season.

Generous applause followed "Nice one, Scottish," Jock stepped in "This team needs some Scottish Iron."

No one put up an argument, not with Jock.

Three, up to the executive suite the lot of you, the Chairman has another surprise,

A two-course meal awaited us, courtesy of our newly extravagant chairman and his wife. We were permitted to have a single glass of wine, tomorrow was matchday after all.

Red Alert

(Vander)

My girls where on high alert, and all my security staff are patrolling the streets to provide them with protection, The Bakker family were providing additional visibility from a distance to emphasise the assurance of safety for the workers of Amsterdam.

Adrianus and I knew that the assailant was far away from Amsterdam, likely location northern France, maybe making his way back to where we suspected was his home, somewhere in the UK, but I couldn't disclose that we had knowledge of the man. The girls were not aware of this information and were distributing the description off the man we knew as the Apparition, between themselves.

Business is Business

(Adrianus)

Rosie is adamant that my connection with The Apparition remains unknown to Maksin, I am not so sure myself, her intel is spot on though.

Evidence against, Maksin is a big player, by now he will know that the quality of the cocaine means high end distribution and not a new kid on the block. That leads to me.

Evidence for, if Maksin was aware that it was my product then he's likely to have made contact, now we are known to each other, to discuss business.

There's a third option, that he does know that it's me but either doesn't want to do business with me or has decided I wouldn't do business with him, the latter is correct of course.

I do like him, but business is business. In this case no-business.

The Hitman and Her

(Maksin)

I am heading back to my HQ in Minsk, my business in Amsterdam being unsuccessful. I don't believe the Bakker family, particularly Adrianus, are open to a trade partnership with our family. Had this been the case they would have been forthcoming with their involvement with our new enemy, The Apparition.

The product is good, the price was good, but not better or cheaper than I can secure elsewhere, with less risk, certainly not worth a family feud, which is not my way of business.

In many respects the use of the go between has achieved the objective, I was able to anonymously broker a deal with the Bakker's to evaluate their openness to a partnership. Walking away from a potential collaboration is acceptable to me, the manner in which my involvement was exposed, is unacceptable. The Apparition must be tracked down and dealt with. It's a matter of honour.

As luck would have it, we've had a break, a slice of lady luck. The professional assassin I had hired, known only as 'J,' and his associate, known only as The Widow who were to intercept a Mr Arnot McCann in Paris have obtained a clue to his identity. My incompetent middle-age tracker had a watch secreted on his person that he had found in Mr McCann's abandoned possessions but had omitted to disclose to me. Whether he would have surrendered the watch voluntarily or not is of little relevance now. He is in no position to say otherwise.

The watch, as I understand from J, is not particularly remarkable or expensive but is believed to be a sentimental piece as it has been engraved on the back with the initials, K. McD. and eight numbers, The Widow believes the numbers to be either a date of birth, a code for something, maybe a safe deposit box, or a bank account. The numbers are not clear enough to make out, but we will know more when the watch has been cleaned.

For now, the information relating to the watch, is not being disclosed to my acquaintances in Amsterdam.

He's no Magnum.

(Rosie)

The trail of The Apparition has gone cold. It's believed he disembarked the train at Lille, but Maksin is not ruling out Brussels. He has no confidence with his tracker's reliability.

No clues, no leads, he'd said. Which means, they have something, but what?

I know of the tracker he chose, a private investigator based in Rotterdam, with links to Amsterdam. A very strange appointment indeed, Ridderkerk PI, was a one-man band that specialised in covert surveillance, predominantly suspected infidelity or monitoring employee conduct, incapacity to work, that sort of thing. People tracking is a bold statement on their website, but Aart Ridderkirk was not renowned for this line of operation.

There were rumours of alcohol and pain killer dependencies, his marriage had broken down, ironically due to her infidelity.

When I think Private Investigator, I think Magnum PI, a dynamic, physically fit, and clever undercover operator with vast resources and technical wizardry to track down and catch wrongdoers. Aart, is none of those things.

Why had Maksin engaged the services of this incompetent, bloated, chain smoking, alcoholic, with a terrible record for success and have us all believe he had one of his best men on the case.

It doesn't make sense, unless he wanted failure to be the result.

Vile

(Kyle)

The hotel is adequate, overlooking Vieux-Lille, the old town. The food was typically French and delicious, as was the wine. I had time to kill, before it was time to kill, my mission in Lille, and the reason for my brief stopover.

My target was still unknown to me, but the instructions had been left in an envelope at the hotel reception desk. There was a map, with a Café La Wilderie circled in red pen. Encased in polystyrene was a vial containing an unknown liquid and a syringe. Finally, there was a sim card.

I was positioned in a courtyard adjacent to the Café, enjoying a crepes suzette and a double espresso, looking the part as a resident of the French city. I had the perfect view of the entrance and the outside dining area of the Café, the establishment had a brisk trade, with patrons occupied in light-hearted discussions, the aroma of coffee and French cigarettes in the air.

The sim card was in the burner phone placed under my napkin, no fingerprints. The phone buzzed.

> *Your target is – white female, five foot five, twenty years old, Light blue blazer with gold-buttons and trim, ¾ denim jeans, white and blue pumps, brown hair tied up under her navy beret, deep pink Batac rucksack. The mark will be leaving Café La Wilderie in 10 minutes.*

I place the napkin back over the message to check the time. Fuck, where is my watch? When did I last have it? Oh no, I can't have, can I?

I must've had my watch when I checked into the hotel, I can't be sure. The last time I saw it was when I took it off on the train to wash my hands. Shit, I can see it there now, by the side of the sink in the restroom in First Class.

Is there a chance that the guy following me didn't find it? I didn't think so, too late to worry about that now, I had a job to finish.

Back in my hotel room now, swiftly packing, cursing my stupidity, the watch, it has my initials on the back, a present from my great-grandfather, his watch originally. No time to dwell as my train to Caen leaves in 20 minutes.

Last check before I go. Sim card destroyed and disposed of, and burner phone gone, check. Vial and syringe in the water around the citadel, check. Envelope and instructions burned. Check.

The job was easy, the girls came out of the café together, my mark was at the back. I stumbled into the other girls, dropped my newspaper and hat in front of them and fell against the railings. While the girls at the front collected my hat and paper, the target assisted me to my feet, as she did, I emptied the content of the syringe into her armpit, which had become exposed by her open jacket.

Initially she had not noticed, but as I turned the corner and looked back, I could see her in some discomfort with her friends forming around her concern etched on their faces.

I had not killed a girl before, I was a little surprised that it had made no difference and that I had not hesitated, not for one second. Surely, killing my wife would be even easier.

Odd socks

(Kirk)

The coach had dropped is all back at Hotel Jimmy, the gaffer said we could stretch our legs and have a walk into the city, but we would to be back and tucked up in our beds at 10:00pm.

This was unexpected, but welcomed, the young lads did not stop for him to reconsider and were off like hares out of a trap. I'll catch you up I shouted down the road, but didn't mean it.

Pat and Jock were discussing whether to have a walk or an early night before the gaffer shouted that Jock was to follow him to plan tactics for tomorrow's game. Strangely they were heading in the direction of a bar.

Pat didn't protest, she shouted after Jock that she had a book to read and would see him later. Geoff was mumbling about odd numbers of socks and what a shit show it all was, just his way of being prepared.

I was left on the corner of the street, billy no mates.

I was going to go after them initially, but I suspected the night would involve debauchery, so I reconsidered my options.

First job, get out of this tracksuit I thought.

Back in the hotel, my friendly receptionist was on the desk. After we'd exchanged some pleasantries, she invited me to join her in her office for a coffee and keep her company. She must have sensed I was about to decline her offer as a wave of disappointment came over her face.

Absolutely, I said, thinking that I still need that alibi. I excused myself temporarily to change my clothes and would return in haste.

As I approached my dorm room, I could hear activity within. Someone was in my room, and it sounded like they were going through our stuff.

I peak my head around the door, you? What are you looking for?

Do I confront her or let it slide?

Pat Burglar

(Kirk)

I feel terrible riffling through Kirk's things, but I have to know whether it was him in the fancy dress, if it was the holdall must be here somewhere. No, nothing here, has he thrown it away.

I hear something outside.

"I'll be back in a minute" I hear a voice, Kirk's voice "I'm just going to get out of these clothes."

I don't think he saw me, as I dash back to my room.

"Pat" Kirk is knocking on my door. I open it tentatively as If I am in a state of undress.

"Yes Kirk, what is it? I am getting dressed for bed" I lie.

"Nothing urgent" he says "It looks like someone's been in my room; I don't think anything's been taken. Did you see anything suspicious?"

"Not a thing, anyone could walk in this place, the airhead on reception wouldn't notice if someone drifted in off the street" I reply. Was the airhead insult over the top I think to myself, too obvious?

"Ok, enjoy your book. I'm going to have a cappuccino with the airhead, if she can heat a drink that is" The smart-arse retorts. That confirms it, I was caught in the act.

I'm not going to sit here feeling sorry for myself, nor am I going to waste my last evening in Amsterdam reading. If Jock wants to spend his time with the gaffer, I will entertain myself, it's not just the lads that can have a good time, I'll go to the blue-light area of the city for a bit of fun of my own.

I'm nervous, but determined and excited. What happens in Amsterdam stays in Amsterdam, I say to myself as I step into the late evening of the city.

It doesn't take me long to find someone that catches my eye, but I walk by, my heart is pounding. I turn the corner and pause to take a breath against a wall.

I head back towards her window and slow my walk as I approach; she sees me and smiles, and I return a smile. This prompts her to open her door and waves me towards her and I involuntarily follow her instruction and before I realise it, I have entered the establishment.

The door is closed, the curtain is pulled across the door to maintain our privacy and she is walking towards me with her arms outstretched to embrace me.

This is it I think, no turning back now, not that I intend to turnback, I'm impressed with my decisiveness.

"What's your name?" she asks

"My name's Pat, Patricia" I reply.

"What do you like to do Patricia? What pleases you?"

I did not hesitate with my response, as she led me to her bed.

Blazers

(Kirk)

The Gaffer designed the experience to be like, to feel the like, an FA Cup Final day.

It was an epic experience, the parts that I can remember, some of it was a bit of a blur.

We knew in advance that we needed to be wearing black trousers. black shoes, and a formal white shirt for match day. What we didn't know is we were to be provided with club Blazers with our club crest on the breast pocket and club ties.

The team members were super impressed, we had thought that this was a bit of a jolly boys outing, a few drinks, not too serious and a token friendly to justify the trip, we were wrong.

The club owners and management had made every effort to impress without bragging and making a big deal of it. Impressive.

At 11:00am we met for the team talk and tactics.

At 12:00 we had our meals, chicken, pasta, beans without sauce. All very professional.

1:30pm was the departure for the stadium. It had all the feeling of a big game, I thought it was a very clever move by the club owners and coaching staff, showing us, what success looks like, preparing us for big games coming in the next season in the highest league level that the club have been involved in in their history.

As we approached the stadium, we could see hundreds of fans walking to the ground and hundreds more in bars near the football ground. This was an under twenty-ones preseason friendly and we were going to have a substantial audience.

At the stadium, the coach parked by the players entrance, and we entered through a guard of honour of home fans waving as we arrived, all very friendly and civilised.

Nervous energy was apparent as we sat in our individual booths under our shirt numbers as we waited in the changing room for the gaffer to give the instruction to change into our strips.

His order was for us to go out onto the football pitch and soak up the atmosphere, the gaffer was impressing me, he had sensed the energy and realise that any words would be lost on us.

I led the team out of the tunnel and into the summer daylight to applause from the awaiting crowd as the stadium compare announced our arrival as the League Champions of Yorkshire, England. Not quite accurate but we smiled and accepted it.

Best team in Yorkshire, said Big Sam and the team laughed with him.

The nerves had evaporated, and we were ready.

Back in the locker room we sat in silence waiting for the gaffer to address us, but it was Jock that spoke first.

His speech was along the lines of, for some of you this will be the biggest game you ever play in, for others this might just motivate you in your football career, but whichever scenario is the one that relates to us we should enjoy the day.

The gaffer reiterated that the most important objective of the day was for us to enjoy it, with a caveat, don't let yourself down as individuals and as a team.

He reminded us of the tactics we had agreed earlier in the day, we would play our own game no matter what tactics Ajax adopted. This was our friendly and we should play as we intend to for the season, play to our strengths.

Graham, AKA Biscuit named after the cracker, Robson, or Robbo as he was known to us, and Ali, just Ali, no need for a cute nickname, were to maintain a compact midfield with Hunter as the anchor.

Robbo and Ali were both skilful and quick, Robbo equally deft with both feet, Ali a lefty. Biscuit had energy to get from box to box and had a fantastic range of passing and an eye for goal. Hunter, AKA Norman, after the Leeds legend, was the steel, but he could play too, he never lost the ball.

Glover, originally had a nickname of Marigold, a tenuous link from glove, somehow he managed to manipulate the name we called him to Goldie, and Donachie known to his teammates as Kebab, Yes Dona-kebab, were young and athletic and were accomplished wingbacks that could overlap Robbo and Ali to provide service to our front two of Dwayne Cooke, ordained to be, Thing One, or T1, and Shabz Hussain. They could defend solidly too.

Thing one and Shabz were strong in the air, T1 in particular. Shabz was lightening quick over a short distance.

We were to play the ball on the ground from the back, Thomas, nickname JT, was reminded to get the ball quickly into the centre of midfield to Biscuit and Norman where much of our footballing industry was created.

I had a few nicknames, Scottish, being the least imaginative, but there was others Big Mac, a McD's reference. Then came McSauce which I quite liked. It was a nickname given to Scott McTominay of Scotland, Man Utd and Napoli and I regarded him as an exceptional footballer and Scottish legend.

When Big Sam Wilcock had the ball, he was to use our other major strength, his huge kicks which pushed the opposition defence further back than was comfortable for them. T1 won everything in the air and his flick-ons to Shabz were devastating for the defence.

Jock reminded us of the strength of our subs bench. Bow, AKA Rickets, and Cook, or Frank, on the basis that he looked like

Frankenstein were utility defenders that could play as centre-backs or full back positions.

Chang, known as Pockets, because he had opposition in his pocket, was our utility player, he could play in defence, midfield and up front, superb energy, and stamina, he could cover every inch of the pitch and never seemed to tire. He was particularly adept at man-man marking, which unfortunately meant he made an ideal substitute. He was the only player in the entire squad that could replace Biscuit, so he was vital to our team.

Singh, or Hughesy after the Man Utd player he resembled on the field of play, gave us another dimension to our attack, his strength was receiving the ball with his back to goal, superhuman strength and outstanding centre of gravity and balance which meant that it was almost impossible to knock him over or off the ball. When we adopted this tactic, it brought on the driving attack from our midfield three.

Most teams were one dimensional with no plan B, or a plan B that were merely desperation by sending hail-Marys into the opposition box rather than a tactic as such.

Leeds Utd's most successful managers in recent years, Marcello Bielsa, was notorious for having only way of playing, plan A, and if that did not work, he would switch it up and play plan A better.

We could pass the ball through midfield, both wings were dangerous, and we could get behind defences and play dangerous balls into our strikers. We could play long balls, and we could mix it up with Hughesy holding it up for midfield runners. When we were on song, we were formidable.

Defensively we were strong, but it was our attacking game for which we were renowned.

Finally, we had Stevie Cooke. twin brother of Dwayne Cooke, he was a straight swap for his brother, but he could also play defence and was our reserve goalkeeper. Another player that had secured his position on the subs bench due to his versatility. His nickname was obviously Thing two, or T2.

Most of the time they were referred to simply as, One and Two.

The gaffer came to us one at a time, clockwise around the locker room, shook our hands and gave us a few words of encouragement. By the time he got to me I was already focussed on the game so all I heard was white noise.

I vaguely recall the referee banging on the door and giving us the two minute warning.

I brought the players together in the middle of the changing room, players shook hands, patted each other on the backs or head and others man hugged. When the time was right, I headed to the door, Pat opened it to let us stream out and she gave me a wink as I passed her.

We formed a line in the tunnel, me at the front, Big Sam behind me and the team behind him. I glanced back to make sure we were all assembled and saw all the players, staring forward, steely focussed. This was my team.

I do not recall the referee walking out and instructing us to follow and it was a blur as we headed to the centre circle, but as we lined up and turned to face the main stand I was struck by the size of the crowd, there must have been ten thousand fans in the stadium.

I shook hands with the AFC Ajax captain, Erik Van der Berg, the match officials, the mascots and the two captains exchanged club pennants. The coin toss confirmed that they had the kick-off.

As I jogged back to my defensive position, I considered what motivation I needed to issue the players, but as I considered their demeanours, I understood that it was not required, each player was focussed and in the zone.

I don't recall much of the first ten minutes of the game, it was frenetic.

On seventeen minutes their number nine, Aarle took the ball thirty yards from goal, Norman was slightly out of position, but certainly not his fault as Aarle struck a thunderbolt that passed a wrongfooted Big Sam Wilcock into the right-hand corner of the net.

Four minutes later it was two nothing, AFC Ajax captain, Van der Berg scored from a well taken free kick, with our keeper having no chance.

Twenty-one minutes gone and we were two down. I gestured to the bench to see if the gaffer wanted to change tactics or formation, but he instead gestured for more of the same.

The next twenty-five minutes were much better, and we were unlucky not to have scored a single goal, it should have been two.

We were incredibly positive at half time; we felt that we were still very much in the game and the scoreline was not reflective of the balance of the game. They had scored two high quality goals, but we had had chances. We were back on the pitch two minutes early, eager to go, Shabz encouraging the team to get him the ball and that he will score he promises.

Two minutes later he had scored, playing high up the pitch on the shoulder of the centre back he latched on to a fabulous through ball by Norman, outpaced the defence and finished smartly with a right foot shot into the bottom left corner over an advancing keeper.

Game on.

It was such a well-orchestrated goal that it had them rattled, they changed their formation from 4-4-2 to a 5-1-3-1 but it did not work, they were outplayed in midfield and although they had additional resources in defence, they gave away the control of midfield and with only one man up front they had limited options in advanced areas of the pitch.

They made five substitutions in an attempt to change the game, we were absolutely dominant but could not get that equalising goal.

We felt that a goal would come for us and stayed true to our footballing beliefs, Rickets replaced JT, Pockets came on for Norman, Goldie made way for Frank, Thing One gave his brother Thing Two, ten minutes of football and Biscuit was sacrificed to give Hughesy an outing.

The changes in personal changed our shape and tactics. With the introduction of an additional forward player, Hughesy who would add an alternative route to goal, and removing a midfielder our 4-1-3-2 had become 4-3-3 with the emphasis on increased attacking options. it was not a gung-ho change, but our control of the game lapsed as we adjusted to the multiple substitutions.

The consequence was that we conceded a very sloppy goal and with 5 minutes of normal time to go found ourselves 3-1 in arrears despite our dominance in the game.

I instructed Big Sam to go down and get medical treatment to give me the opening to give a team talk.

The message was simple, we were a good team, we had played well, we had five minutes plus injury time to get back into the game. We were not going to accept defeat, let us push for the next goal and see where that takes us was my rallying cry.

The talk worked, a long ball from Big Sam, flicked on by Thing 2, which hit Shabz on his shoulder and with the instinct of a sniper, he executed a deadly left foot volley into the roof of the net before the goalkeeper could react.

It was still 3-2 to AFC Ajax and they had decided that their tactic was to frustrate us by keeping the ball, it was working too.

I made the decision that we were either going to lose 4-2 or get that equaliser, it was a friendly game, so no genuine jeopardy existed.

Deep into the 8 minutes of injury time to be played, the ball was sent along the ground to the left wing, Ali flicked the ball around the corner to the overlapping Kebab, Kebab drove to the byline and presented a magnificent, chipped cross that Shabz tucked away with a neat header at the far post.

Shabz Hussain had scored the perfect hat-trick, right-foot, left-foot, and a header, we were all square.

We had previously agreed that there would be no extra time, but that the game should have a winner as a result. Penalties would follow.

Shabz despatched the first penalty, they then equalised. Hughesy almost burst the net and then scored again also, 2-2. Pockets scored as did Robbo and we led 4-3.

One of their subs missed his penalty and it was my turn, If I scored, we win, if I missed then they will have the opportunity to draw the penalty shootout and force sudden death.

When I stepped up for my penalty, I was feeling relaxed and calm. I had decided on my walk from the halfway line that I was going to hit the ball low and hard, the lower the goalie has to dive the harder it is for them to get to the ball before it passes them. But which side? I decided that I was going to arch my run to give the appearance that I was going to wrap my right foot around it and aim for the goalkeepers right, but that I will put it in the other corner with a hip swivel if he moves to go right.

I did not change my mind as I placed the ball on the penalty spot. I looked at the Keeper and he was giving nothing away, bouncing on his toes, but as I started my run towards the ball he stepped to the left and gave a bigger target to his right and was pointing for me to hit the ball in the bigger gap. It was tempting and an easier shot than swivelling to change my body shape. As I arched the run he moved back to the right and then athletically flung himself to his right, his right glove making it all the way to his right-hand post before my shot arrived at the goal.

Fortunately, my shot was to the opposite corner and as he landed and rolled onto his haunches, I was heading back to the centre spot with fifteen players charging towards me to celebrate wildly.

Final Score

AFC Ajax　　　　　3 - 3　　Holbeck United

HT 2-0

Aarle (17, 85)　　　　　　　Hussain
Van der Berg (21)　　　　　(47, 87, 90+7)

Holbeck United win on penalties 5 – 3.

Overlord

(Kyle)

I stand overlooking the British Channel, imaging the hundreds of tiny boats advancing on the Normandy sand I am now standing on. Contemplating the horror that awaited those men and the fear of death that would have surrounded them.

My great grandad had been one of those many servicemen who invaded Gold and Sword beaches along with the might of the allied forces.

I have come to pay my respect to the man I did not know, on the 80th anniversary of that military operation that will be remembered forever more in the history books. The man who gave me his watch with his initials and the date 06061944 engraved on the back, initials that I share being named after him and the date of the D-day landing.

I was devastated to have lost his watch, but maybe that was how it was meant to be. I was holding his watch until I could visit his resting place.

On my way back to Caen, I passed the 'For your Tomorrow' silhouette art display, a poignant and moving tribute to those men who laid down their lives for our freedom.

I allowed the thought that I had wasted my liberty and all my opportunities, like so many ungrateful and undeserving of current humanity, I allowed those thoughts to consume me, for a moment, I deserve to feel this way.

On the ferry from Cherbourg to Poole, I ponder my current life in Edinburgh and the wheels that are in motion now to bring about the changes I intend manufacture.

The chosen route back to Britain may seem unusual for a man who had escaped the gangsters, who have been trailing him, somewhere between Brussels and Paris.

They may have had men watching the ports of Calais and Oostende, I think it's possible, but they would not send their soldiers as far west as this.

Significantly and importantly is that they don't know who they are looking for.

The Urban Myth
(Kirk)

A return to the sex club was the plan for the lads, the Cooke twins had taken the stage at Casa the previous night to the delight of the crowds and the club owners. News had spread quickly throughout the streets of Amsterdam that male twins were going to take to the stage with either one of the club staff or a willing female customer.

The club was standing room only apparently to see the act, the twins had entered the stage from opposite ends and the Compere had asked the audience if there was a lady in the audience that wanted to collaborate with them.

Three ladies had come forward, so their names were placed in a hat. Sharon, Shaz, a 45-year-old woman from South Shields was chosen and took no time in stripping naked and laying on the revolving bed on the stage, and the twins took no time joining her in a frenzy of sexual activity.

As the team assemble at the first bar, there is chatter about the story involving a guy on his stag party who is invited to the stage by a female performer and is tied up and assaulted. The story never happened. it's an urban myth, but a story lads like to tell, nevertheless.

I was telling my own made-up story, that Pat had advised me to take a short walk to stretch my hamstring and then I had to rest up, so I made my excuses to avoid the sex club again.

Hunted

(Kirk)

I stretched my legs in the direction of the Hotel Ibis, and the lovely Lucy. We had not arranged anything, but I thought I would take my chances and see if she had been abandoned by Becky again.

As I pass the Flying Dutchman Pub, I see the girls through the window engaged in conversation with a couple of guys, looking all cosy sharing a couple of bottles of wine, so I decide to double back and see if I can find the rest of the football team in the Red-Light district.

I am surprised that I feel slightly jealous and pause for a second and consider heading back to the pub and ordering a beer at the bar and see if she notices me. I decide that's childish; she is on a trip away with her friend so is free to do as she likes.

I head down Nieuwendijk street which I think is the general direction of where I need to be. Down some of the side streets to my left I see it looks livelier, so I decide to take the next left. Now I know where I am, directly in front of me is the Grasshopper, not far now.

I pass the aptly named Dirty Dick pub and navigate my way to Oudezijds Voorburgwal where I recall us finding ourselves on the first night and the Bulldog finale for me. I am aware that the strip club is across the canal and onto Oudezijds Achterburgwal a little further down the road.

The streets are seedier than I remember, and there appears to be groups of men on every street corner. Some looking like they are homeless seeking handouts, other who are peddling in drugs, but there are some serious looking brutes, which were definitely not apparent the other night.

The atmosphere in the streets around the Red-Light area seem eerie somehow, and I am feeling uncomfortable.

I seem to be drawing attention to myself, so I take a seat on a set of stone steps, adjacent to The Old Sailor Pub overlooking the canal to gather myself, are people really watching me or is this my imagination?

Caught in the web.

(Rosie)

My encrypted devices start to buzz, three alerts from Voodoo via the dark web. All sightings of our Apparition, how can this be possible?

Sightings at the Grasshopper, near Dirty Dicks and outside The Bulldog. Last seen heading down Oudekennissteeg. They lost him on Oudezijds Achterburgwal heading in the direction of Casa Rosso.

Voodoo is at Casa Rosso with a welcoming committee, Dusk-Shadow is enroute, ETA 10 minutes.

The boys and I are in the car, we will be there in 6 minutes.

Hello Sailor

(Kirk)

There is something occurring this evening in the city of Amsterdam, I can feel it, a couple of black Range Rovers pass me by, with purpose. The posse of gangsters who were gathering in number outside The Sailors Pub are now all making their way in the direction where the cars are headed.

I have a feeling that the situation is more serious than a bit of tourists' high jinks, I decide to hide within the pub they have vacated and observe for a while.

The chatter within the bar is speculation surrounding the gang or family that the gangsters were affiliated to; the names mean nothing to me. One of the doormen had allegedly disclosed to the bar staff that there has been an assault on one of the working girls and that there have been sightings of the man.

The description is not known but there is a rumour that they are looking for a British man.

Tonight, has been a bust, from start to finish. Starting with Pat going through my belongings, presumably looking for something to connect me to the mystery man in fancy dress. Next, I stumble upon Lucy with another fella and then my reluctant jaunt to catch up with the rest of the team, sees me walk into a manhunt. I am calling it a night.

Leaving on a jet plane.

(Rosie)

The welcoming committee provided by Vander and Adrianus' crew had Cassa Rossa under surveillance for hours, with no result.

They had sent out search parties in pairs, to scour the streets, with no success.

If The Apparition had returned to Amsterdam he had vanished again.

The man who went by the name Vander, Adrianus and I were sat at the rear of an authentic Dutch restaurant that had been closed to the public since we had arrived. Our security teams were monitoring the perimeter of the premises.

I had explained to the pair that my information on The Apparition was that he was in France, destination the UK. What means of transport he was using or which route and under what alias, was unknown.

If there had been sighting of someone who matched his description, which I doubted, it was not our ghost.

Vander agreed that the sightings were not the man we were looking for but had suggested that the excitement of the evening would work in his favour. The girls were encouraged by the show of strength we had displayed.

Adrianus had news too, that Maksin, had moved his operation out of Amsterdam.

My business is concluded in Amsterdam, I tell them, and I am leaving tonight. What I fail to tell them is that I am heading to Lille on the trail of The Apparition who is believed to have murdered a young student. Somone is sending me their private jet, so I imagine the murdered girl is a family member or friend of someone important.

Klingons to the starboard bow

(Kirk)

"This is your captain speaking; we are awaiting two final passengers that have just passed through security checks" was the announcement from the cockpit.

The two seats to the side of me were empty. Bex and Lucy I guessed were the two passengers we were waiting on.

"The plane is not delayed; we will be departing on time" announced the captain.

"Before I hand over to our amazing flight crew, I want to say a warm welcome to this flight to a fellow captain, Captain Kirk, of Holbeck United FC."

Here we go!

"We are just checking that there are no Klingons on our starboard bow, but don't worry the ground crew have their phasers set to kill."

Oh, how the passengers laughed.

"In all seriousness, Kirk, congratulations to you and your team for defeating Ajaz FC on penalties, following what I understand to be a thrilling 3-3 draw, and we have it on good authority that you scored the winning penalty".

Cheers and applause rang round the plane as the seatbelt signs illuminated and then a second round of applause erupted as the two mortified girls boarded the front of aircraft to begin their walk of shame to the very back of the plane.

Bex attempts to push ahead of Lucy so she can sit next to me, but as she is stowing her bag in the overhead lockers Lucy jumps across the seats in a flash and has her seatbelt fastened.

"Hello handsome" says Lucy "Good to see you again."

"I didn't think you were going to make it" I replied.

"Enjoyable trip?" I ask, with a wink.

"There was a particular highlight" she giggles.

Bex stares forward, arms folded, clearly vexed with her friend's decisive manoeuvre.

"How was your football match?" Lucy enquires with a cheeky smile. "Did you win?"

"Yes, we did win, you've just missed the captain waxing lyrical about yours truly here" I add prodding my own chest.

"Really, what have I missed?"

As we taxi to the runway I tell her about the game, the goal, the penalty, commemorative jersey, and the tour of the stadium while she nods and smiles while faking interest in my football story.

Once we are in the air, the hostess leans over the two girls and says "Mr Shatner, you are needed in the bridge" and disappears to her trolley duties proud of her little joke.

As I head to the cockpit, I glance back to see the girls in heated debate. Lucy will have to tell her.

The captain greets me at the cabin door and shakes my hand vigorously. "I follow Garforth Town, myself" he says "Local club, for a local boy, not so much a boy nowadays" he offers.

I would guess late fifty's early sixties.

"Heart Of Midlothian, the very same reason" I respond, I have not been to Tynecastle stadium for too long, I think to myself.

As we enter, there is a hand on my shoulder and someone pushing past me. Without invitation, there is the gaffer requesting to sit in the co-pilots seat. If I am the captain, he must be the Admiral and has taken charge.

As I arrive back at my seat Bex is sat in my seat by the window and a rather sheepish, Lucy is sat in the aisle seat.

"You don't mind being the rose between to thorns, do you?" says Becky.

"Not at all, it sounds very comfortable" I lie, feeling like I am, a gazelle being pinned down by a couple of lionesses. I give Lucy's arm a reassuring squeeze as I shuffle into my seat.

Becky links her arm around my arm and says aloud "Let us share holiday stories, we will go first, won't we Lucy. Not that Lucy let her hair down like I did" she cackles.

I smile at Lucy and mouth; it'll be ok.

Becky begins to regale me with their activities over the past few days, stories designed to make her look good and Lucy a little less so. I was beginning to dislike Rebecca. I am sure Bex and Lucy are good friends really, this is all a big show for me, Bex the dominant one and her loyal friend Lucy, a perfect match. I assume Bex is used to getting her own way and Lucy is the peacemaker.

I'm wise enough not to give my dislike for her away, that would not impress Lucy.

The stories are monotonous, 'we got so drunk, we met these boys' was the repetitive main theme. They visited the sex museum and sex shows and sat on the front row to get a closer intimate view. They had to see what the red-light district was all about; they had had space cake and got the munchies and discovered the most amazing kebabs. I had to admit that the kebabs in Amsterdam were especially good.

More stories about drink and guys that they'd met, yet she was at pains to clarify that neither Lucy nor Bex had 'got off' with any of the guys they'd met, but I knew that not to be true. The reason that they'd not taken anything further than a bit of harmless flirtation with the boys they met came as a bit of a surprise. Bex was celibate, she meant she was abstaining from sex currently, I doubted this information also. But the big shock was the announcement that Lucy not only had a boyfriend back in Halifax but was due to be engaged.

There was one quite amusing story, that I think I got most of the detail correctly. A coach trip of middle-aged British couples were spending the day in Amsterdam on a tour of cities, we were guessing Paris and Brussels being the others.

Anyway, at some point a few of the party had separated from the main party as they were on a guided trip of the city centre, and despite several frantic telephone calls they could not be located.

The tour guide, a very tall, slim Dutch gentleman with a green scarf attached to a long pole announced to the party that the missing tourist had the itinerary and would no doubt be heading to the national monument and Dam Square. The group agreed and followed behind, a matter of seconds later there was huge commotion, and two red faced, potbellied, men emerged from the fracas and hurried away down the main drag, followed very closely by two angry women, shouting and screaming at the shamed pair who had been caught red handed leaving the same young lady's business premises.

We said our goodbye's as they left the plane, Lucy a little embarrassed and couldn't maintain eye contact. I'd not expected to learn about her impending engagement, which had been a gut-wrenching revelation.

As I was waiting at the taxi rank in the pouring rain outside Leeds/Bradford airport, thinking as I always do, why Leeds shares an airport with Bradford and why both councils agreed to build the airport on top of this bloody hill? I see Bex approaching, closely followed by Lucy, and without a word she pushes a piece of paper into my hand and scurries away to a waiting car.

When I am in the safety of my taxi, I unfold the cheque sized document to discover a coupon. The coupon has two telephone numbers connected in a cross the sixth number in each of the telephone numbers

sharing a zero, and underneath the words –
Three's company, we'll book the hotel room.

Flame Grilled

(Kirk)

The lads had in fact snuck off to visit a sex show on the eve of our big friendly match, I suppose it was a walk of sorts, which had given me the window I needed to visit Lucy's hotel.

I'd anticipated that she would not be there, but I intended to leave her a message. I'd contemplated calling her friend but had decided that this would be problematic.

There was no bar at the Ibis Styles, very much a budget hotel I found. Not quite as basic as our accommodation, but basic, nevertheless.

I was about to leave a message with reception when I spotted Lucy sat outside the hotel entrance on some extremely uncomfortable looking red metal chairs. I wondered whether I had missed her on my way in.

"Hello" I said, louder than I meant to, which made her jump and drop the mobile phone at which she was staring.

"Oh, Hi, this is a nice surprise" she replied without missing beat.

I sensed a confidence I had not seen on our brief flight from the UK, she looked beautiful in the early evening light.

Her beautiful skin glowing in the sunshine, dressed in an orange jump suit, accessorised with a brown and orange patterned scarf, brown bag and shoes and sunglasses.

Her hair was long with flowing curls, flashes of copper highlights catching the curves like waves breaking.

If she's wearing makeup which is very subtle, maybe a little eyeshadow and some lipstick, but I would suggest that was it.

"Are you waiting for Rebecca" I asked.

"No, she's met someone, I've been on my own most of today" she says.

"Mind if I join you?" I say while grabbing the back of one of the heavy metal chairs.

"Please" she says and pours me a glass of wine from the bottle she has in front of her.

"I'll have a small one" I protest "Big game tomorrow."

I discover that her friend had met a guy the previous night, had a cheeky snog and exchanged numbers. Then at lunchtime today, Bex had insisted that they had lunch in the beer garden at the Grasshopper and low and behold there was the guy from the previous night. Her friend had asked Lucy if she minded entertaining herself for the afternoon for a few hours, which was over 6 hours ago.

"Have you eaten?" I enquired.

"No, I'm starting to get hangry" she laughs.

A term I have not heard before, but I guess it's a state where hunger leads to angry agitation.

"There's a steak restaurant, just up the road" and I point to Central Station "Unless you are vegetarian/vegan?"

I wonder if I have said something wrong, she had paused and give me the once over.

"You are full of surprises, Kirk, how did you figure that I'm of Jamaican heritage?" she says, linking her arm up with me and setting off towards the steakhouse at pace.

I take the compliment without truly knowing what I've done to deserve the praise. I soon learn that Rastafarianism, a religious and social movement, developed in Jamaica in the 1930 has a strict diet, eating only the freshest and most natural foods. Meat is considered as dead food and Rastas observe the no bone zone rule.

Apparently, my observation that Lucy was Jamaican and could be a Rastafarian and therefore vegetarian or vegan was major triumph. I decide it will serve no purpose for me to come clean.

I learned that her grandparents on her mother's side had emigrated from Jamaica in the 1950s, encouraged by the British government to cover the labour shortage. They'd lived on a fabulously named Dolphin Island on the south of the island, near Mitchell Town.

Both her grandparents had worked for the NHS and lived in Leeds. Her mother was also born in Leeds in the sixties but moved to Halifax when she met her father. Her mum was a schoolteacher until her retirement.

Her father had visited the UK in the early 1980s, initially to travel, he loved football and cricket and the popularity of both sports in England had him hooked. He was accepted into university and secured a job in Halifax after he had graduated where he worked all his working life until he retired at age 60, a few years ago.

I'd ordered the T-bone steak, with all the fixings, she had ordered the tenderloin, in a Diane sauce, with salad instead of chips.

Despite my match the following day I had ordered a beer and a bottle of Argentinian Malbec for us both. She'd requested sparling water for two without checking that worked for me. I was not insulted; I prefer sparking water and like her confidence.

She told me that her parents would like me, which caught me off guard a little, she must have noticed my cues and recovered by saying that family was important to her, and she always judged men based on whether her parents would like them.

I liked her honesty and openness, but I did wonder whether they would approve her bringing home a white boy and not a nice Jamaican suiter.

There was not a single clue that she had a boyfriend and was set to agree to marry him.

It was now almost 9:30pm and seemingly no word from her friend, Bex, so she texted her to say that she hoped Becky was having fun, and not to worry about her and that she was entertaining herself sightseeing, that she was going on a guided tour, including a boat trip, and would see her back at the hotel at midnight.

We skipped dessert, opting for a coffee, we both take our coffee black, no sugar.

After a perfectly lovely meal, we took a walk along the canals, and then we walked back to her hotel.

I politely kissed her cheek at the hotel doors and agreed that we would see each other again. She held my hand and pulled me close again and suggested that we could visit her room together. I used the match as an excuse to decline her invitation, but it didn't sit comfortably.

She lingers to give me the opportunity to reconsider, which I do, but I know the right thing is not to visit her room tonight. Maybe tomorrow night, I think to myself, but I don't ask her or make any arrangements, which I regret immediately.

See you on the plane we would both say as we part company.

Boyfriend, engagement? I thought we had something. Had I kidded myself that we had had a special evening? Why had she lied and kept the boyfriend a secret.

I will probably never know, another encounter to put down to experience.

Part Two
Edinburgh

FR E SH A VOCA DO

(Isla)

I'm making breakfast. Today it's avocado with poached egg on a warm muffin for me, and soft-boiled egg and sourdough toast soldiers for our children Maisie and Hamish.

As usual, we, the McDoyle family are in a morning rush, I have the children to drop off at Kyle's parents before I need to head off to work.

Kyle's mother, Rita, often offers to provide breakfast at their house in Georgie, to ease the morning turmoil at the McD's household before my commute to work, our home is a short distance to their home in the west end of Edinburgh.

If their son, Kyle, would pull his weight that would be he helpful, but they focus on the wife responsibilities, so I alone am left to raise our children. Ted and Rita pick up the slack that their useless son abandons.

I enjoy breakfast with the children even though it's frantic, it's important to me that the family day starts off with us together, plus breakfast at Grandma's would be some sort of sugary cereal, probably with chocolate.

Kyle, my husband, is still away on a business trip. Business trip? Unlikely, more like some dodgy deal no doubt, one day there will be a knock at the door, and he will be taken away by the Scottish Police. I hate living like this I think to myself, our children deserve better, I deserve better.

I enjoy my job as Head of Human Resources, for one of the four universities in the city. We are currently consulting with unions regarding the inevitable restructure which includes a substantial risk of redundancies in both the academic sphere and in professional services. There are no areas of the university that are unaffected by the current cost cutting requirements.

Our universities in Scotland are not as impacted as south of the border, we are government funded and not as reliant on the tuition fees as universities are in England and Wales. However, funding is not meeting our current needs so cuts to spending and staff job losses are being considered.

My Husband has not had a proper job in forever, he had a job when we first met, we fell in love, and we were married.

When I fell pregnant with Maisie he started to spend more time at the gym, then came the use of steroids, his circle of friends changed, and he started picking up weekend night shifts as a doorman.

He packed in his day job and was sleeping all day and in the evening, he was either at the gym or working the pub and nightclub doors of Edinburgh city centre.

There were rumours of other women, and enough evidence to suggest that the rumours were true.

There were spells when I moved back in with my parents, but then he would agree to change his ways, and we would start over. Each time I hoped, but without much belief, that this time would be different, it never was. I was afraid of being a single parent, and I wanted our unborn child to have a father. I thought that once he was father, he would adopt some responsibility. I was naive and foolish.

He was a handsome man, he still is in truth, he has always taken care of his body, maybe a little too much. He has become vain and arrogant and any love between us has gone. Living together is like a business arrangement, a very one-sided business arrangement.

If he is frequenting other women's beds, that just makes it easier for us. It's not an element of our relationship that I miss.

He's not particularly good in bed, so I don't miss the sex. I miss being close to someone and feeling love and being loved but the sex I do not miss.

I had a reasonable sex life before I met Kyle, so I know the difference between good and bad sex.

I thought that intimacy and familiarity would improve our love life over time, particularly once we were married, but it didn't improve. He didn't really try, not genuinely, he just wanted to satisfy himself, and that ridiculous tongue thing he does when giving oral, I had to fake an orgasm just to make him stop.

I have never actually had an orgasm with Kyle, I should never have pretended to in the first place, it was a mistake.

I'm not sure that I've ever had a proper orgasm with anyone, it has been nice, but not the mind-blowing experience I've read or heard about.

You don't miss something you've never had I remind myself.

Can of Worms

(Kyle)

Five thousand euros deposited in my secret safety deposit box, in a well know high street bank. The proceeds of my deal in Amsterdam.

I have a further two thousand euros that I took from the twenty thousand I delivered to the Insomnia Coffee Shop. It was an error on their part not to have the barman, Pieter, count it.

The ridiculous, theatrical, fighter pilot, come B.A. Baracus, fancy dress outfit had worked a treat. I'd wondered whether the excessive jewellery was a little too much, I needn't have worried.

I'd known the garish look would demand a change of clothes, in fact the need to change out of my Top Gun outfit would signal that the deal was on and that there were no unexpected hiccups.

The detour to Café Van Beeren had giving me the opportunity to change and therefore help myself to a couple of bundles of twenties.

I doubted that they would check the bag during the exchange, or at all. The money would either be back in the food chain or as part of a larger stash of cash, either way, they wouldn't notice a few thousand euros were absent.

After I've changed the Euros into Sterling I will give Isla, my wife, a thousand pounds, for the family coffers. This will evidence at least, as far as I was concerned, that this was a successful business trip. The amount that is left will all be for me.

I hadn't been paid for my job in Lille, there would usually be an arrangement in place where I would receive half before and half after the job is done, but I was already in debt to an associate of the contractor. I agreed therefore, to complete the job and wipe the debt.

A successful trip indeed, I think to myself as I enjoy a Laphroaig, single malt whiskey and a lager chaser at the Shandon, snooker and pool hall, a bit of easy money.

I could have used the five thousand euros to pay off some debt but, who to pay first? Also, where I got the money would be a question that I could never answer. Not without opening a can of worms.

I'd had a look into two drug gangs' businesses and ruffled some feathers. No one would suspect the involvement of Kyle from Dalry.

I'd hoped that asking for train tickets to Edinburgh would work as a double bluff and keep them away from my city. Once I had departed the train to Paris and left the identity of Mr Arnott McCann behind, surely, they would consider that Edinburgh was the last place they should look for The Apparition.

Swing Low

(Kirk)

Dear Mr TenderloinXXL,

I trust that our arrangement in Amsterdam was satisfactory, I have another engagement for you to consider, in Edinburgh tomorrow. Further details will follow if this liaison is acceptable to you.

Regards

Rx

The message had come through to my personal profile on the website swing2uk.com, as had the previous contact from Rx, or who I now know to be Rosie Sparx.

Initially I had explored the swinging scene out of curiosity but then it became a business opportunity as a male escort.

The website was not for escorts, either male or female, but it became a place where I could be contacted anonymously and secretly by clients. Recently my clients had become more exclusive and discretion more important. I replied.

> Dear Rosie,
>
> Amsterdam was as expected, similar arrangements for Edinburgh are acceptable.
>
> Regards T

No explicit talk of sex for money here on this site, my profile would be shut down if there was the merest hint of commercial enterprise, this site was for consenting adults offering free love.

Witching Hour

(Rosie)

Admiring the view of the magnificent walls of Edinburgh Castle from my suite in the Witchery Hotel, I contemplated the imminent meeting with Mr Tenderloin and the secret assignation arranged with a lady member of parliament for Scotland.

It wasn't for me to investigate who had committed the most terrible of crimes in Amsterdam, I'm a fixer, and I occasionally share information I have obtained, for a reasonable fee of course. A platinum standard fixer, with a worldwide reputation for discretion and strict confidentiality.

My identity was known to many, but no one knew my clients, and I will be keeping it that way.

I don't want to believe that the spectacularly stunning Mr Tenderloin was the perpetrator of the crime, he was in Amsterdam to meet the American Actress, as per the arrangement I had set up. The other man was in Amsterdam, quite by coincidence it would seem, to do business with my clients Maksin and Adrianus.

At this stage I'm not ruling out that they are one and the same person, but there must be another explanation.

Did our Mr T have a brother, maybe a twin brother? She realised that she didn't know anything about him. She had tried to glean where his hometown was when the first met in Club Deluxe, but he had not given anything away.

What she did know about him is that he was extremely talented and in high demand, and he was going to make her a lot of money.

Double Cross

(Adrianus)

'Ping' Unknown number.

Mr Apparition,

Mission successful.

Maksin has moved his operation out of Amsterdam, I have acquired his business interests here. An added bonus, caused by your antics in the city centre, has meant that Vander is too pre-occupied with the security of his people to branch out into my business concerns.

Pieter, as you suspected, was working with Maksin, he let slip that you had returned to Edinburgh. Only Maksin, Vander and I knew that your train destination was Edinburgh.

You are exceptionally good Mr Apparition, you also predicted that he would help himself to some of the money, around ten percent you estimated, and you were correct again.

He has confessed to a number of deceptions and double-crossing under mild interrogation.

He will no longer be a problem, thanks to you exposing our mole.

You played the fool well, Pieter did not suspect a thing, I was not so sure about your fancy dress plan, but it was inspired.

Maksin has contacts in Edinburgh, my intelligence suggests that he has set up a meet to enquire about you.

Stay safe my friend.

A package has been left for you with the concierge at the Balmoral Hotel containing your final payment and new phone.

Destroy your current phone and sim card, now!

Adrianus

He who laughs last.

(Adrianus)

'Ping'

> *Warning appreciated; I am not in Scotland. Location classified. I will send a revised location for final payment when safe.*

"Can I get you anything Boss," said the barman.

"Yes, Pieter, you can get me one of those milkshakes of yours" I said.

I did not believe for one moment that Pieter was working with Maksin, and I anticipated the temptation for our Apparition to take some of the money.

That is why I did not ask Pieter to check the money. The money was not important if it helped me uncover the identity of the Apparition.

I needed The Apparition to think Pieter was dead and that he had got away with taking the money. Plus, my friend, there is something about Pieter, that you could not have known.

He who laughs last laughs the loudest Mr Ghost.

Bullshit

(Kyle)

I don't buy any of it. The text message from Adrianus is all bullshit.

Too much detail pertaining to the two thousand euros. You would not be concerned with a missing two thousand euros and speculating that I'm in Edinburgh, very clumsy Adrianus, very clumsy indeed.

Too much praise and admiration, what is your game?

Pieter did not take the money, I did, and I am convinced you know that, so the torture and murder of Pieter is all a lie.

Why did you feel the need to make me think that Pieter was dead?

I'm on my guard now. Full alert.

Who is Vander?

Why did Adrianus reference a person I don't know, is this a threat?

Thinking on my feet.

A Wee dram

(Kirk)

Balmoral Hotel, 7:30pm.

Ask the reception to connect you to a Mr Steele.

These were the instructions from Rosie. Café Royal was going to be my first stop for some Scottish fare and a wee dram of whiskey, single malt, just a wee one as I don't want to hamper my performance.

Impossible

(Kyle)

I'm leaning against the Wellington Monument, on Princes Street, opposite the Balmoral Hotel, disguised as a Big Red Bus Operative, the perfect disguise in Edinburgh. Everyone sees me but everyone looks away, not wanting to make eye contact just in case I approach them for a sale.

I see the two Russian security guys from Maksin's hotel suite, they are leaving the Balmoral Hotel entrance. The Footman opens the limousine door for them and the Russians disappear inside while the car speeds off to an unknown destination.

The airport is my guess.

Now I know that it is Adrianus that has sent these goons for me. Your message was too obvious Adrianus

As I'm sat in the Guilford Arms with a double whiskey and threat, I wonder whether Adrianus and indeed, Maksin, believe I am in Edinburgh, or do they conclude that my request for a train ticket to the Scottish capital was a bluff and that I'm in a location unknown?

Out of the corner of my eye I spot him passing the pub window on West Registry Street.

"That's impossible" I say aloud.

Waterloo

(Rosie)

The man known to her as The Apparition, is not in Edinburgh, he would surely have collected his final payment if he were here.

The other alias's he has been known by, he discards and leaves no trace remaining. They certainly do not lead a trail to Edinburgh.

It was convenient that I'm here with Vladimir and Vladimir, AKA, Bert, and Ernie, as I lovingly refer to them, to meet Mr T and another of my clients. I therefore agreed to a business proposal from Adrianus to conduct a sting on The Apparition.

Bert and Ernie arrived at the Balmoral Hotel early, they had the receptionist, and the footman appraised of the situation and had provided them with a description of the man that they were looking for. They left a package with reception with the instruction that they should contact them should he come asking for it.

They kept a close watch on both entrances with no success.

They'd anticipated that if he were watching the hotel that he would walk by the entrance or engage in conversation with the footman before committing to enter the building, neither occurred.

A perfect spot for keeping watch on the Balmoral would have been from the statue of a soldier on a horse directly opposite the hotel.

Bert had told Ernie that the significance of statue of a horse posed with the two front legs off the ground was that the rider had died in battle. A statue where the horse has one leg raised signified that the rider was wounded in battle.

Ernie was certain that the statue was that of the Duke of Wellington, who won the battle of

Waterloo against Napolean's French legions, this statue has the horse with two legs off the ground, yet this soldier didn't die in battle. So, Bert must be setting up a punchline to a joke, Ernie had deduced.

"What is the significance of all four legs of the ground?" Bert had asked.

"Oh, God" Ernie had exclaimed with despair.

"Horse is Circus Horse" Bert laughs.

"Terrible" says Ernie.

That would've been the best spot to watch the hotel they both agree, but there was only one of those guys in a Big Red Bus uniform, selling bus tours. We stayed away from him they told me.

I report back to that the trap has not worked.

We were unclear what we should do if he had turned up to collect the package. We're not gangsters; we do not work for gangsters; we do not engage in criminal activity. I am a fixer, I provide information about people, I find people and I arrange confidential meetings and rendezvous between willing parties.

Ghostbusters

(Adrianus)

So, the Apparition is not in Scotland. It was not a double bluff after all, it was a long shot, but it was worth a punt with Rosie and her henchmen in Edinburgh, fixing things, or whatever she is doing there.

Yes, I knew you were in Scotland Rosie, I have my sources too.

As for you Mr Ghost, our business is not concluded, if you should reappear to spook me again, I will be forced to conduct some Ghostbusting.

Tourist Botherer

(Kyle)

There he is, sat at the bar of The Café Royal, musing with his whiskey in his hand. I had not been mistaken; he could be my twin brother.

We don't look alike right now, not with me disguised as tourist botherer, but if you saw him at a party, you could mistake us for each other, easily.

He's dressed to impress, very smart indeed, smart casual they would call it these days, maybe. I would guess that he's having a stiffener, a bit of liquid courage, before a date.

I start to get that strange feeling that I had in Amsterdam, I want to move but I can't. My hands and body feel as though someone else has control of them, I see my reflection in the window, and it starts to distort into an image of a laughing devil, and in an instant is gone.

My hand involuntarily moves to my face as if raising a glass to my mouth and I can taste whiskey.

Snap out of, I cry out internally, and I am back staring at my human replica. This phenomenon must have been sent to me as an opportunity, but an opportunity for what?

I have no need for a look-a-like, I have no wish for a brother, twin or otherwise, but there is a strange feeling that it is our destiny to meet, fate has sent you to me.

I take a few steps back and rest against the railings adjacent to the entrance of the bar, today has been stressful I agree with myself. Forces are trying to close in on me, is this another trap?

I have time on my hands, I will observe my subject from a distance and follow him for a while.

Going Up.
(Kirk)

I break from my hypnotised state, how long was I staring at my glass of whiskey, I don't recall finishing it, but there it is, an empty glass.

"Another one?" says the bartender.

"I don't remember having this one" I mutter.

"Are ya waiting fe someone" she enquires "You've been staring oot that windie like."

I check my watch, and it says twenty past seven, I've lost about ten minutes, I'd checked the time when the drinks came, and it had just reached ten past.

What was I doing staring out of the window for ten minutes? and why can I not remember finishing my drink?

No time to dwell on my situation now, I have an appointment with the fixer and a mystery lady.

What were those instructions again, so not to upset those bodyguards of hers? Who was I to ask for?

'Whack'

"I am so sorry; I wasn't watching where I was going" I apologised.

I've just flattened one of those Red Bus salesmen, his clipboard and leaflets are strewn across the cobbled road, and he's in a heap on the ground.

"Let me help you" I say as I help him to his feet.

"I'm ok, just a little dazed" he says, I get a hybrid Irish accent, I think. "You in a rush Sir?"

"Aye" is my honest response "Are you Ok?"

"I will be, on you go, you have places to be, it's not the worst assault I've suffered in this uniform, hazard of the job" he chortles.

"At least let me help you pick up your leaflets" I insist.

"You go on your way, go see your girl. It is a girl is it not" and we both laugh.

Happy fella I thought as, I head across the street to the Balmoral Hotel, I wonder if he has a facial scar or something, he wouldn't let me see his face.

"Mr Steel's room please" I ask at the desk.

"One moment, Sir" the receptionist replies

"I have a gentleman in the lobby to see a Mr Steele" she says into the telephone, and "I'll connect you now."

I'm directed to go and sit in the corner of reception where another telephone sits.

"Mr T?" says the voice on the other end.

"Mr T, take the lift to the penthouse suit" Click.

The Bellboy's been informed in advance that I'm visiting the penthouse, and it would appear that he's been instructed not to make eye contact or engage in conversation.

Do I give the boy a tip, I ask myself?

My wallet, where's my wallet? I must have left it on the bar at the Café Royal, too late now, I'll have to collect it after my appointment.

Lucky Fucker

(Rosie)

"Boss" says Bert.

"Reception called again; she says the man heading up in the lift shares the description of the man who was due to collect the package earlier today."

"Hmm" is my response.

"I told lady receptionist that it was ok" Bert finished.

"I believe that the soft approach is called for, a female touch, we don't want you two big lumps scaring our money maker away. I'll handle this" Is my response when I should have thanked Bert.

"Sit down please Mr T" I say, in an incredibly soft and friendly manner.

"Now, we cannot continue this Mr T nonsense can we, and I'm certainly not going to call you Tenderloin or XXL for that matter" I laugh.

"I'm Rosie, and you are? Just your first name will do" I did not want him to think this was an interrogation.

"Kirk"

"I'm, Kirk McDonnel, from Leeds, formally of Edinburgh, Scotland" he said which stunned me for a moment.

"I don't need to know, nor do I want to know any more details about you, Rosie will suffice" he added.

"Very well, Kirk" I smiled.

"Would you like any more information about me Rosie? I assume you have enough to carry out some background checks" Kirk adds.

"I would give you my date of birth, but I don't know it, not my real one anyway" Kirk offers with a shrug.

"I appreciate that you're introducing me to influential people, your clients, which require confidentialities, so in the spirit of trust and transparency, on top of the NDAs I'm willing to continue to sign, you can carry out all the due diligence on me that you need"

Clever and gorgeous I say to myself.

"I'm sorry you won't find anything exciting though Rosie, not unless you like antiques, or watching poor football" he jokes.

I rather like him, I say to myself, but I must control those urges.

I smile and laugh with him.

"I appreciate the gesture of trust and will of course reciprocate, as far as I can you understand."

"In lieu of the ongoing circle of trust we now share, can you tell me, did you travel back to the UK by train immediately after we last met?" I enquire. Will this be the moment of truth, or lies?

"I think you already know the answer to that Rosie, I'm sure your driver told you that I didn't go to the train station" He replies.

"I'd like to hear it from you" I insist.

"No, I didn't head back to Leeds immediately after we met, I had further business in Amsterdam to address" was his reply.

I saw my boys sit forward in their chairs.

"Go on" I urge.

"I was in Amsterdam for two reasons, one was to meet you and your client and two, I was in Amsterdam with my football team to play a friendly match against Ajax."

"I flew home curtesy of KLM Airways, and not the train." Kirk says, with a wink to the boys that I later understand.

"Wait" says Ernie.

"You played at Johan Cruyff Arena?" he continues.

"Yes" Kirk replies.

"Holly Shit, you are a lucky fucker" Bert says jumping out of his seat.

"I heard about this game" adds Ernie "an amateur team from England gave Ajax pros a real tough game."

"It was only their under twenty-ones" Kirk adds.

"Enough" I say to the boys, "you cheerleaders can talk sports later, we have business."

Bert and Ernie sit back down and start to giggle and pinch each other like schoolboys that have been scolded, and I roll my eyes at them for added dramatics.

"That explains it, Kirk" I say.

"One final question, on your lads' football trip, did you have a fancy-dress night out."

"Fancy dress?" I say, "No, why?"

"No matter" I say.

"Wait, Rosie, has this anything to do with a Top Gun Pilot?" Kirk asks, and he seems very intense.

"What do you know about that?" I say.

"Apparently some of the lads bumped into someone that looked like me in the Grasshopper, dressed as you describe" Kirk explains.

"What time was that" I say.

"Eleven thirty to eleven forty-five" he guessed "The lads were meeting for one last drink at eleven thirty."

"You were in my limo at that time" I state.

"Yes, yes I was" he says.

"Our driver says he dropped you near the hotel Ibis around ten to twelve" I say.

"That sounds about right" he says, "Lads arrived back just before midnight, and I was already there, ready for role call."

"What is all this about" Kirk implores "Who is this guy you are looking for?"

"Better that you don't know" Bert chips in

"Inconvenience to our business" adds Ernie.

"Don't concern yourself, Kirk, you have work to do" I remind him.

"Now, sign this" and I pass him the NDA.

I tell him to knock and enter through the door in the corner and remind him that Bert and Ernie will ensure that they are not disturbed and will ensure he gets to his hotel. I assumed he was staying in a hotel and not heading back to Leeds, and he confirmed that he was.

There is much to be done, I will start with those background checks, find a date of birth and family. I suspect he has a brother, probably a twin, that he is not telling us about.

He's from Edinburgh, which is convenient for my investigation.

Not my first rodeo

(Kirk)

As I enter the Penthouse suite, I pause to gather myself, my mind is occupied with questions regarding my conversation with Rosie. Who is the mystery man that resembles me and what has he done to demand such interest?

I must put aside the thoughts for the next hour or two.

In the sitting room there is a gentleman reading a newspaper, he glances briefly over the top of the rag and tosses his eyes in the direction of a set of double doors. I see he has an earpiece and a wire and take him for her security guard.

I knock and enter, she's waiting in the centre of a king-sized bed, under the covers and propped up slightly by and additional pillow. I take off my jacket and introduce myself.

"No introductions" she says in a broad accent.

"You may recognise me" she adds "but I see no benefit in me confirming who I am, if I later must be compelled to deny it"

I don't entirely follow her logic, but I am not here for a high brow debate.

In the corner by the window is a man seated facing the lady in the bed, he's wearing only a small towel over his lap. He smiles politely and then looks over at the lady.

"You don't mind if my husband remains in the room do you?" she asks, and they exchange a smile.

"No madam, I do not" is my response "Should I take a shower"

"Yes" the man says.

"Indeed" She agrees "but don't close the door, we'd like to watch"

And they did.

In my early days when I first joined the adult dating, swinging scene I had realised that there were very few single females searching for single men.

There were many married couples where the husband would experience pleasure from watching his wife enjoy the company of other men. In most cases the men would join in if their fantasy was for two men at the same time. There were some couples where the husband preferred multiple men taking it in turns, and there were those that just liked to watch. At first the voyeurs unnerved me, but later I began to prefer this scenario, particularly if the wife ignored that her husband was there at all.

There were occasions when the husband would join his wife after we had finished, and that was fine with me, it gave me a reason to go on my way and leave them to it.

It was when parties were where I was mostly in demand, that I became more comfortable with being watched performing, so being watched having a shower did not pose any problem.

It was slightly off putting when they both wanted to dry me off, especially when the husband was paying more attention to the tender areas of my body than she was.

I'm not a small man, so it was difficult for them to position me on the bed, but it was acutely apparent that they wanted me to lay on the bed so that she could take control.

Once they had me where they wanted me, angled for optimum view from the husband's vantage point by the window, she began.

She began to use her mouth to explore my chest, stomach and my shaft while cupping and squeezing my balls. All the while her husband watched eagerly, maintaining an engrossed expression with his little towel covering his lap showing a slight bulge.

As she continued to lick and suck, her eyes remained fixed on her husband, she was putting on show for him.

Kneeling up, she used her arm to measure my length and girth which caused her man to gasp, before she lowered herself on to me and began to rock and gyrate, performing like a cowboy at a rodeo, all the time keeping her eyes fixed on her husband.

She took her pleasure, shared her pleasure with her husband, I was just a means to an end, but I was being paid well, so didn't care.

As our encounter was about to come to an end, she called him over and he came up from behind her and began to massage her breasts causing her to climax another time, I followed shortly after and slid out from under them, leaving them to kiss and caress each other.

I vacated the room without them noticing I was leaving.

Rest Easy

(Kyle)

Kirk McDonnel of Leeds, nice to meet you. The contents of your wallet proved most helpful, providing me with the preliminary information to progress my plan and yes, I now know why fate has brought you to me and what purpose will be served. First to return your wallet to you.

"Hi, is that the Premier Inn at Haymarket" I enquire.

"Yes Sir"

"Do you have Mr McDonnel staying with you?" I ask.

"I am sorry Sir; we do not provide details of residents. I cannot neither confirm nor deny whether Mr McDonnel is staying here" the telephonist responds.

"Of course, I understand, it's just that I have found his wallet in the street with a keycard for Premier Inn and receipts from your bar."

"If I give you my mobile telephone number, can you ask Mr McDonnel to contact me, so that I can return his wallet, thank you" and I hang up, and wait.

Room 101

This is damn inconvenient; I'll have to report my card lost or stolen. What else was in my wallet?

Driver's license, bloody hell, how much will that cost me to replace? sixty quid? I did not have much cash in there, forty pounds at the most. That will be gone, even if my wallet is found.

"Hi, I am staying in room 101" I tell the young guy on reception.

"How can I help you Sir?" he replies.

"I've lost my wallet, containing my room keycard" I speak.

"Mr McDonnel?" he enquires.

"Yes, that is impressive" I say, "How did you know that?"

"A gentleman called earlier, he's found your wallet in the street and has traced some of the contents back to this hotel, Mr McDonnel. His name is Kyle and here's his telephone number, he must be a decent guy to be wanting to return your wallet" The young receptionist explains.

The thirty-nine steps

(Kirk)

We agreed to meet at the Mercat Bar and Kitchen in the Haymarket area of Edinburgh, for me to collect my wallet, which was not too far from my hotel. I had offered to treat Kyle to a Scottish breakfast and a cold Guinness for his trouble.

He's late though, it's almost ten thirty and we agreed to meet at ten, I'm about to call him when I receive a text message.

> *Running a bit late, kids to blame. Have breakfast and I will meet you in your hotel reception at twelve.*

I ordered the house breakfast and a Guinness, though refrained from adding the eight-ounce steak available as an option.

My waitress, Niamh, is a lovely Irish lady, I would guess late twenties, could be thirty. She has strawberry blonde hair styled in a bob, held back with an incredibly attractive headscarf and has sparkling, emerald, green eyes. I guessed that the choice of black skirt and white shirt was one made by the establishment as a simple uniform. She has pulled off the look, wearing her skirt not too long and not too short, accessorised with a half black apron. Her white blouse, with an extra button left unfastened that boasts her attractive neckline and a teasing hint of cleavage.

She tells me that she's a mature student at the local university, studying fashion and design, with an ambition to have her own line of children's clothing. She's working at the Mercat part time to help with the bills. I suspect that she's probably a single mum, but she hasn't disclosed that level of information.

The breakfast was outstanding, in particular the haggis and the Lorne square sausage.

There was only Niamh and I in the bar by the time I had finished my food, the Chef had taken a break, to the bookies, which was apparently his thing.

I ordered a second Guinness and drank it sat on a bar stool chatting with Niamh as she prepared the bar for the lunchtime rush.

I paid for my meal with apple pay but had no cash to give her a tip, so I promised I would return and leave a five-pound note with her manager once I had my wallet returned.

On the receipt she gave me she added her telephone number and scribbled a little note to me which said 'You could just to bring it to my place x'

I would certainly think about it.

Out in the street the air hit me, two pints of Guinness before lunchtime is maybe not the best idea I have ever had.

"Hi Kirk, let us have a walk" says a fella in a high-vis jacket, hard hat and dust mask.

"I'm Kyle by the way, and here is your wallet" he says has he holds the wallet in front of me.

We keep walking until we are in the grounds of the Cathedral Church of St Mary, and we take a seat on a bench overlooking the grounds.

"What's with all the thirty-nine steps style espionage, Kyle?" I say, thinking back to a book I read at school, and a decent play too if I recall.

"Thanks for my wallet by the way" I add.

He removes his hard hat and dust mask, and all becomes clear.

"What the fuck is going on" I say to Kyle as I start to laugh involuntarily.

"First, let me say what a bloody handsome guy you are, and secondly, what the fuck?" I continue.

"I wouldn't say we are identical; but I would say that only my mother would not be fooled" Kyle replies.

"Jeez, I'm a little bit in shock!" I say.

"I was too, when I first laid eyes on you. I thought I was hallucinating!" Kyle replied, placing his head in his hands.

"When was that, exactly?" I enquire.

"Yesterday. You walked past the Guilford Arms on your way to the Café Royal" he replies without lifting his head.

"Red Bus man, you fucker!" I say, standing up from the bench and pacing up and down.

"Yes" Kyle replies

"Why all the fucking disguises?" I demand to know.

"No disguises" he says "I do odd jobs here and there, wherever I can get work really. A bit of groundwork, labouring, doors at a pub and club, tourist stuff when the money is good, anything that sees me paid on wages day"

"What do you do, Kirk, where in the world are you from?" Kyle enquires.

"I work in antiques, in a little town called Huddersfield in Yorkshire" I reply, I have no idea why I said Huddersfield, it just came to me.

"You don't look like the type to be wearing a waistcoat, cravat and a monocle" he says.

"I'm one of those contemporary dealers, not much call for fancy outfits in Yorkshire, I do sometimes wear a flat cap" I joke "Anyway, you are the one with a penchant for fancy dress."

Then it hits me.

"Wait, were you in Amsterdam recently?" I ask and I watch closely for his reaction.

"Where? Is that Holland? Not me Kirk, I couldn't go there even if I wanted to. I don't own a passport; I don't feel the need. The furthest I travel outside Scotland is Newcastle."

He didn't flinch, either he's an extremely accomplished liar, or it really wasn't him.

"Cards on the table" says Kyle, very matter of fact and decisive.

"I have a job for you, interested?" he says but it does not sound much like a question. "Before you say no, know two things, one; it's nothing illegal, you just have to pretend to be me for an evening and two; the job pays well. What do you say?"

"I'm listening" I respond, but I have no intention of doing it.

"I've been double booked. I'm working the doors at The Worlds End and Mrs Kyle has booked a night out at the theatre and a nice meal. I was supposed to have booked the night off work months ago, but I forgot and now it's too late to take time off work."

"Can you not swap shifts with a mate or take your Mrs out another night.?" I check.

"Nah, I can't let either down, I am in a real pickle. My marriage is in a rough place as it is, knife edge to be honest, and my boss doesn't exactly follow employment law, if you get me."

"OK, what are we talking? Five hundred pounds?" I ask, half joking.

"If you shake on it now, I will give you that five hundred pounds now and another five hundred when it's done" he replies holding out his hand to shake.

"Let me think on it" I say.

"You would be helping a brother out" he says, looking rather desperate.

"I'm heading back to Yorkshire tomorrow; you'll have my answer before I leave.

£1,000 for one evening's work, there is something not right. What is the saying? if it sounds too good to be true, it probable is.

Uddersville

(kyle)

Why did Kirk say he was from Uddersville, or wherever he said?

I took the opportunity to sneak in his hotel room, while he was in the Mercat. I did have his room key after all and who was going to challenge his look-a-like?

I know all about you Mr Kirk McDonnel of Leeds.

High-Class

(Rosie)

Kirk is who he says he is, I've had him checked out.

He was adopted, birth parents and actual date of birth have been erased by someone extremely powerful. There are absolutely no records.

He was raised by a Mr and Mrs McDonnel, Angus, and Morag, know to locals as Gus and Mo.

Gus and Mo were successful in the adoption after a long and arduous, vetting and interview process.

They did very well out of the deal, along with the job came a house, two competitive salaries and access to a substantial trust fund, through a very reputable and highly esteemed Advocate, Mr Castel.

Kirk's education had been provided for by the trust fund up to leaving university and he stopped receiving money from that trust fund at twenty-one years old.

His adopted parents have had no contact with him since he was eighteen when he moved to Leeds for university, they have emigrated and now live in Costa Brava, Spain.

Kirk has done OK for himself, according to my contacts in Leeds, he was gifted property in a will and has an established a pawn business.

The business is not so successful, he is buying more than he sells.

No girlfriend.

Few Friends.

Joined the adult dating, swinging site Swing2uk just over three years ago under the profile name TenderloinXXL.

His initial profile had an image of him sat at a bar, in the sunshine abroad somewhere holding a beer, and he was seeking females only. Presumably instead of having a girlfriend.

Later the profile picture was changed to that of a semi-naked image, seeking females and couples, as he became more adventurous. There were also pictures of his endowment for site members only.

The current profile is considerably basic, there is a picture of him in a suit with a glass of something fizzy. Available for party's and special liaisons it says, and there is an extensive list of recommendations and positive comments left by satisfied connections.

He has built quite the name with the free love swinging community.

Initially, he was paid expenses to travel to meet exclusive members and to attend parties, as his reputation grew, he began to receive a fee to attend parties and to escort.

His fame has propelled him into the escort scene as the most in demand exclusive high-class male escort in the UK.

This is where I was made aware of his particular set of skills and began to receive requests to broker a rendezvous with my A-list female clients.

He is an amateur footballer and his football team, Holbeck United FC really did visit Amsterdam to play a charity match with FC Ajax.

His passport was used as he disclosed, on flights in and out of Amsterdam.

He is not The Apparition.

His Doppelganger exists though, but who is he and where is he?

Simples

(Kirk)

I can't claim that it wasn't a weird encounter in the grounds of the beautiful church, I don't really know what to make of it.

I want to forget about it, but I'm intrigued to pursue it to learn more about you.

What are the chances of two people that look almost identical and born in the same city, not being from the same biological parents?

I've not been interested in looking into my biological parents before now. I've wondered from time to time whether I have brothers and sisters, I think I'd like to have a little sister.

A brother, not so much, certainly not Kyle who seems to be a bit of a dick.

The thing is, the uneasy feelings that I had in the shower and in the limousine in Amsterdam, returned in the church yard when I was with him, almost identical feelings that I was not going to let him know about.' Then there was the experience I had in the Café Royal, in front of the barmaid, where I blacked out for ten minutes. Kyle was lurking outside then too. He has to be the cause of these paranormal feelings; I don't believe that he was not in Amsterdam.

Now that I have my wallet, I can give the incredibly attractive Niamh another visit and make good on my promise to give her a tip.

The Mercat is significantly busier than it was for breakfast service, I was contemplating having a late lunch and chatting with Niamh to get to know some more about her, but it doesn't look like that will be possible.

I spot a space at the bar. If she is available, I think to myself, I will have a drink and a bar snack.

"Niamh, here is your tip from earlier" I say, with a smile as I approach the bar "I'll have another Guinness please."

Niamh smiles broadly as I approach.

"Kyle? What the bloody hell are you doing here? are you following me?" The lady with Niamh shouts towards me.

"Do you two know each other, Mrs McDoyle?" says Niamh.

"No, I don't know this man" she screams and marches past, knocking into me as she goes by.

"Him? He's a complete stranger to me" she shouts back as she leaves the bar.

"That was strange" says Niamh.

"Maybe I initially looked familiar? I'd better go after her, can I call you later? I ask.

"Yes, call me!" Niamh shouts as the bar door closes behind me.

I catch her up just before Ryrie's bar on her way to Haymarket train station.

"I think I know who you think I am" I say, "I'm not Kyle, and I can prove it."

Green Eyed Monster

(Isla)

We talked a lot, we had a lot in common, he was charming, interesting, and funny.

This certainly was not Kyle. I'd actually realised that it wasn't Kyle at Haymarket station and had agreed to back with him to Ryrie's for a drink out of curiosity.

Kirk's eyes are both a brilliant electric blue, which remind me of the Mediterranean Sea, whereas Kyle has one blue eye and one a greenish, grey colour.

Kyle's eyes are dull, almost milky, devoid of life behind them, while Kirk's eyes are bright and alive, sparkling, and brilliant, like deep pools of water, enticing me to dive in.

There are other differences as well as Kyle's heterochromia that set the men apart. Kirk is articulate and intelligent, caring, and friendly.

Kirk and Kyle may look similar but looks are where the similarities end.

I couldn't think of a time when I had felt more comfortable with a man, the conversation flowed. There was no subject for which he could not provide imaginative insight, balanced views, opposing, yet considered arguments or fascinating perspectives.

He listened as I talked, he genuinely listened and was interested, he asked appropriate questions to clarify his understanding which showed that he was interested in what I had to say, he was interested in me.

I want this man.

I thought to myself what a stroke of luck it was having to call in on our student, Niamh, she had been missing lectures and her attendance was beginning to show as a red flag on our welfare reports.

I had agreed to call in to her part time place of work, because it was next to my solicitor's office in Haymarket, where I had an appointment booked to see what could be done to remove Kyle from any claim to my inheritance and make a financial agreement to separate if we could.

That's why I'd reacted badly when Kirk approached me, I'd thought that Kyle had been following me to and from the solicitor's office.

The trip had been a success, good news from my solicitor, I had also been able to provide Niamh with support for her financial struggles through the Student Finance Team and the Student Union, and I had met a quite remarkable man.

Free Hit

(Kyle)

'Ping'

> *Kyle, I'll do the doors for you for one night only. No payment required. One good deed for another, you returned my wallet I will help you mend your marriage.*
>
> *Kirk*

That's the news I wanted.

Now, I must plan this meticulously, I have one chance at this, while you are being me, I will take care of her.

Then unfortunately my brother, I will need to take care of you. You are the only possible witness, the only person that could destroy my alibi.

You look like me, that is all, I have no feelings towards you, we are not friends, we are not family. I am using you for a job.

Being near you makes me feel strange, unearthly. In the church gardens I had the same reoccurring feeling I had when I saw you through the window of the bar. I had that feeling before in Amsterdam and I suspect, from your questions in relation to Amsterdam, that you were in Amsterdam too, and that you're having the same hallucinations and paralysis as I am when we are in the same vicinity as each other.

Once the grisly job is done, I'll end the feeling that an evil spirit is possessing me, when I end you.

If everything goes to plan, Kirk will be implicated in Isla's murder too.

China girl

(Kirk)

I text Niamh, I was a bit fresh, an old Yorkshire term to mean slightly drunk.

I probably wouldn't have contacted her if I hadn't had a drink though.

She replied straight away and was still at work, so I met her there. She was very pleased to see me, and immediately embraced me, a little too eagerly.

Several customers were watching us, so I gathered that she'd told some of them about my imminent arrival, her fellow barmaid gave her a thumbs up and blew a kiss.

We had a pleasant walk to her house, in the old town, which as it turned out it was not so much a house, more of a flat, called The Snug.

The Snug was hidden away down a side street, the door was an old oak door which appeared to lead to nowhere in particular. Inside, the room that greeted us was no larger than a small sitting room, which looked a little like a gentleman's smoking room or a small library or study in a large house. But this was the main room.

The walls were made of oak panelling and a mixture of real and fake bookshelves. Behind a curtain was a small kitchen with a breakfast bar and behind a fake bookcase was a small bathroom comprising of a toilet, shower, and a sink.

The apartment was small but functional and I actually quite liked that it was quirky. Where was the bedroom though? I was soon to find out.

Niamh poured us a glass of white wine each, tucked the bottle under her arm and led me through another tiny bookcase, which took us up a tight staircase above the study and kitchen.

We had to crawl into a small space that it transpired was a double bed with less than three feet of headroom.

This place was weird and fantastic.

Removing our clothes was a challenge and we clashed heads more than few times, once disrobed we laid there a while slightly out of breath, and we began to laugh.

I wondered why someone had designed a room like an indoor VW camper van, made mostly from wood.

Even though there was insufficient lighting, it was still clear enough to discover that her skin was as white as the most delicate porcelain, and smooth to the touch.

Our laughter disappeared as we began to take things seriously. I was feeling the effects of afternoon drinking though and found I wanted a sleep more than I wanted sex. Despite the bed being like a bunk bed it was incredibly comfortable.

I was given a reprieve in the way of a brief disco nap when she decided that she needed a shower to freshen up.

Housekeeping

(Kirk)

I'd arrived back from Niamh's place in time for the hotel breakfast and wished I'd have gone to the Mercat instead.

I'm not saying the hotel breakfast was bad, but it wasn't good. There was no Chef on duty, so the cooking was left to two young staff members, it was overcooked, lukewarm and dry. The bacon had the texture of beef jerky.

I could have had the continental breakfast but that's not really a breakfast in my opinion.

A freshly cooked English, Scottish and even an Irish breakfast for that matter is in comparison gourmet to that of a hotel buffet style breakfast. The Mercat breakfast is the epitome of this culinary breakfast finery.

I had expected breakfast at Niamh's, but as it turned out, it wasn't actually Niamh's place at all. She lived near the University, not in the old town, The Snug was a rental property that she cleaned on Sunday mornings, she knew it was empty this weekend and had always wanted to spend the night there.

I needed sleep. After my initial snooze while she showered, Niamh had kept me awake all night, mostly talking, but only while she was recharging her energy for another round of sex. She claimed that she had 'not had any' for a while so was making up for it. Make up for it she certainly did.

I was correct in assuming that she was a single parent, which is why she didn't want to take me to her place. Her mum was babysitting for her daughter, Sorcha, who was almost 5 years old, and had beautiful red hair and was a mini-image of her beautiful mum, Niamh.

I had negotiated a rate to have a late checkout at 2pm, which would allow me a few hours' sleep and then I was heading up Dalry Road for the match.

I was packed, showered and had just lowered myself into bed, when there was a knock on the door.

"I have a late checkout" I shouted

Another knock

"later!" I shouted

"No understand" came the reply in what was maybe a Polish accent.

I opened the door wearing only a towel around my waist, ready to try to explain calmly, but calm I was not.

There stood Isla, in a long coat, carrying a holdall. My first thought was that she had left Kyle, my next thought was how did she find me? and third was, wow.

She had untied the belt of her coat and opened it, revealing that she was wearing only stockings, suspenders and lacy black underwear with killer heals, underneath her coat.

She looked incredible.

I was pushed back into the room, she didn't wait to be invited, threw her bag by the bathroom door, dropped her coat to the floor while simultaneously closing the hotel room door.

"Order Housekeeping?" she said, in the rather bad Polish accent. The door must have muffled just how bad it was.

I stepped back to sit on the bed, but as I did, she grabbed me, preventing me from doing so, removed my towel and flung it in the direction of her bag.

"Don't say a word, before I come to my senses and change my mind" she said.

"Kiss me" she whispered.

So, I did.

Afternoon Delight

(Isla)

I had never been so nervous or so excited in my life. After leaving Kirk the afternoon before I had decided I was going to seduce him. It was a feeling that was all consuming.

So, I headed to Victoria's secret and spent far too much money on seductive underwear I could scarcely afford, on a whim.

I had felt sexier in the changing room in the store off Leith Street, than I had throughout my entire marriage.

I had almost turned back several times, and my legs almost gave way in the hotel lift,

It had worked though, Kirk's face when I loosened my coat was a sight to behold. I'd experienced a series of exquisite pulsations or 'fanny flutters' as a result.

Kyle is not a good lover, my boyfriends before him were ok, but I'd never had an orgasm with a man.

I'd never experienced much foreplay either, when my friends talked about it, I just went along with the conversation. Sex was mostly painful with Kyle, because I was never stimulated enough to be ready for sex.

With Kirk it was different, we kissed and caressed each other for several minutes, then he concentrated his attention to my most intimate of areas, teasing and softly stroking at first, then a little firmer.

He was very skilled with his fingers, as he explored me the feeling was incredibly intense.

He then began to kiss my body all over, starting at my neck and shoulders, then my back, bottom and legs, before turning me over and commencing the kissing again, at the front this time.

His exquisite mouth and tongue made their way between my legs and at first, I froze expecting the worst, but unlike Kyle, this was not rushed, there was no lapping dog technique or twirling tongue.

Soft, delicate brushes of his tongue, building in pressure and intensity overwhelmed me, it was incredible and that was when I had my first earth shattering orgasm of the evening and my first ever with a man.

As I regained my composure and breathing, I admired his magnificent body as he kneeled in front of me, his huge erect penis ready for me, I feel nervous that it will hurt, a lot.

As he slides gently in me, I do not feel uncomfortable pain, for the first time I am ready, and it feels incredibly good.

The sex is by far the greatest I've ever had, and I have at least two more orgasms, it might have been three, but they were so close together it could have been one continuous climax.

I lay there exhausted and satisfied while he has a shower.

I suddenly feel the urge to feel high again, so I open the shower door kneel in front of him and start gently and rhythmically licking round the tip of his huge penis. I have never been a fan of giving oral sex but the urge to pleasure Kirk is undeniable.

He did not come during sex, and I was too busy with my own agenda to take control and make it happen.

I was going to make it happen now, he is huge and difficult to handle, I hold it with both hands and eagerly give head, taking as much as I can in my mouth whilst massaging his balls and the base of the shaft.

He tries to pull me away as he starts to come, but I want to taste him, so I wrap my mouth around his cock again and feel him explode.

I have been reborn.

Tynie Arms

(Kirk)

It was to be her first football match, not a particularly romantic setting for a date but, the match was one of the reasons I was visiting.

The captain on the plane had reminded me of my hometown club, so I had decided that I would take in a game when I could.

As is my tradition when I go to a match, we had a couple of pints in the Tynecastle Arms before the game, then a quick dram before departing for a walk around to the other side of the stadium to take our seats in the Roseburn stand. I was impressed that Isla had joined me in having a pint and a wee whiskey.

The home end is the Georgie stand, situated behind the goal opposite Roseburn. The Main stand and the Wheatfield stand, which are either side of the pitch housed the rest of the home fans. I preferred the Roseburn stand, and don't know why, I thought to myself, maybe habit.

Once in the stadium I ordered us both a Scotch pie and a Bovril, she had considered ordering a macaroni pie but decided that we would have the same. If this wasn't our first date, was it a date? I would have offered to split the pies. I'm partial to a macaroni pie myself, but you can't beat a peppery, meaty scotch pie on match day.

Isla appeared to be enjoying herself, the Tynie Arms had been incredibly busy, but we had found seats away in the corner, I draped my Scarf around her neck, and she gripped it tightly as if it were a prise position and someone might steal it. She clapped along to some of the songs and watched the rapturous singing by the fans with fascination in the pub. She abstained from the more risqué and indecent songs.

She linked arms on the brisk walk to the turnstiles and smiled enthusiastically as she soaked in the atmosphere outside the stadium.

Once inside it took her a few minutes to take it all in, a football stadium is a strange place, intimidating, enthralling and exciting all rolled into one. Like a huge theatre with the audience anticipating the actor's entrance and the expectation of an exceptional performance.

As can happen in the early games of a season, both teams are a little nervy, a little rusty. Passes are not as accurate as they should be, the strikers lack that extra yard of pace it seems and are less than clinical in front of goal. The game feels wide open though and is exciting for both sets of fans as a result.

Hearts are playing towards the Roseburn end in the first half, and we are treated to goal scoring chances but as the clock ticks down in the first half it is looking like both teams will head in at half time nil, nil or nothing each as it is referred to up in Scotland.

Rangers defenders must be thinking the same as they pass the ball between themselves with little urgency. Their midfield general drops back into the defensive zone to collect the ball, he turns and drives forward and into midfield, he hits a strong pass attempting to split the Hearts defence but it ricochets' off the back heel of one of his own men into the path of the Hearts number ten, who plays a first time pass diagonally into space on the left hand side. The pass is perfectly weighted for the left winger to burst past the defence, take a touch, look up and see the Hearts number nine arriving at the back post. The ball is delivered into the box, inch perfect, the goalkeeper is stranded as the Hearts forward powers a diving header into the top corner of the net.

The striker runs towards the stand that we are in and performs a knee slide in front of us and is consumed by his teammates in a heap on the turf.

Isla takes the opportunity to fling her arms around me as she jumps around with the ecstatic fans and plants a big kiss on me, to my surprise, but I like it.

The second half is very much like the first half, lots of energy and ambition but without any real quality or either team taking control.

On sixty minutes Hearts have a corner, and our big number five wins a towering headed duel and fires the ball towards goal, I cannot see whether the goalkeeper stopped it or whether it hit the post, but it rebounded into the centre of the penalty box, there was another shot, which was blocked, then another blocked shot. Oohs and aahs repeated for what felt like an eternity before cheers rang out from the home end and Hearts players reeled around and headed back to the centre of the pitch celebrating.

More hugs and kisses.

There were a couple of half chances after that, but as the game entered the last five minutes, both managers made substitutions reminiscent of a chess game, the Rangers manager would make a substitution to change the formation or tactics, then the Hearts manager would counter with a substitution of his own to 'check', another substitution 'check' again. Finally, the referee blew his whistle and that was that 'checkmate,' Hearts had won two-nil.

Pinball wizard

(Isla)

My first football match had ended two nil to Hearts.

It was an exciting match, or so Kirk had told me, I tried to get involved but football is not for me. I like Kirk, so I listened to his football stories but no, I will not be rushing back.

Although there was an interesting advantage to be had when his team scored. Everyone jumps around hugging and kissing each other, there doesn't appear to be any boundaries or rules, so I took the opportunity to grab myself a kiss or two. It felt very naughty but, very nice.

After the match we walked back to his hotel to collect his luggage from reception and headed to the train station. We shared an enthusiastic and passionate kiss before he boarded the LNER train back to Leeds, and that was that. A brief but exhilarating encounter, I doubted that I would ever see him again.

As I waved him away, I turned and straightened myself up. I felt like a new woman, with renewed purpose, things needed to be said, things needed to be done, but the timing of it would be critical.

I also had news for Kyle from the solicitors.

Van-der

(Vander)

This is not my first time in Edinburgh, but it's been eight years or more, I've placed over one hundred young ladies here from all over Eastern Europe, they're all doing well I hear. I'm not known as Vander here though. Here in Scotland, I am known as the Dutchman.

"Business or pleasure, Sir" enquires border Police.

My business is pleasure, I saved myself from saying. Instead, I smiled to myself.

"Leisure" I said, "I'm an historian, I'm researching the Clans. Mac's and Mc's are fascinating to me, as are the tartans they wear."

I think I lost her at the word 'leisure'.

I am being partially truthful, I'm looking for a Mac, a particular Mc, with the initials K. McD.

The information was not too expensive, and I wasn't too perturbed that the update wasn't provided by Maksin as had been our agreement. It was Rosie that had contacted me with the information relating to our Mr Apparition, leaving his engraved watch on the train. The intelligence had been gleaned from the dark web Electra had advised. I suspected that she had discovered this information on her trip to Lille, when she had been summoned to assist in the murder of a young student.

With my passport stamped I was on my way through passport control to collect my luggage.

Adrianus would have to cope without his second in command and expert milkshake provider for a few days.

Pieter Van der Beek, I said to myself you look more like a geography teacher than an historian.

Only Rosie and Adrianus, know that I am both Pieter and Vander. I am known as Pieter to most, famous for my milkshakes, a chosen few know me as Vander, even less know that 'Van der' in Pieter Van der Beek is where Vander is hidden.

Part Three
Leeds

Decisions-Decisions

(Kirk)

After the excitement of the last few days in Edinburgh, I decided to take some time to relax in the tranquillity of my orangery, in my detached house, on the grounds of the old St Mary's Hospital in the West region Leeds.

The orangery isn't as grand as it sounds. It is a conservatory with brick walls, and I don't store my tropical fruit there either.

The house left for me in Rabby's will is just five minutes' drive from my pawn shop business and fifteen minutes from Leeds city centre, with convenient access to the M1 and M62 motorways.

Now I'm home I'm thinking about Isla, Niamh, and Lucy. Specifically, I am thinking about settling down. In the space of a few weeks, I've met three amazing women, yet all of them are unattainable. Lucy is promised to be married, Isla is married, although unhappily and Niamh, is focussed on her university studies and not looking for a relationship, certainly not one that would mean leaving Scotland.

I love Leeds, I love Yorkshire and Yorkshire people, 'Gods own Country' they would declare, and I feel what they feel. Yorkshire is beautiful. The locals are fiercely loyal to their region, and straight talking. Residents of Scotland and Yorkshire folk have many shared similarities.

I feel like an honorary Loiner, a citizen of Leeds.

Leeds is the capital of Yorkshire, and one of the fastest growing cities in Europe. It's also fast becoming the second most important UK city for financial services outside London.

Geographically it's situated in the centre of the UK, two hundred and twenty miles from the capital of England, London, and two hundred and ten miles from the capital of

Scotland, Edinburgh. It's also less than fifty miles from Manchester, connected by the M62 motorway and extensive railway links.

Decision one is made, I am staying in Leeds.

Decision two. I write on my pad, 'stay or go'. Am I staying in this house or is it time to sell up and have a fresh start?

I draw two columns, in the left I write 'pros' and in the right column I write 'cons'. I sit in silence for a while then I write across both columns, 'This decision depends on whether I will be living alone or whether I will be with someone, maybe start a family'.

I agree that this is a perfect family home, just too big for just me rattling around in it on my own.

Next item, I write 'job' and 'pawnshop'.

If I am honest with myself, the pawnshop is not a business, I'm not making any profit, I take a wage and not a very good wage some weeks.

Not that I need a lot of money, I own the building so the overheads are low, I don't have a mortgage either.

I wonder how much the buildings and businesses are worth, but if I sold them what would I do.

I had hoped to be a professional footballer, but my abilities had fallen short of what was needed, so that plan had been shelved many years ago.

I conclude that I am thinking too much and that a massive decision like this needs time and due consideration.

Before I put my pad down, I write 'partner-wife' and subconsciously add 'Lucy'.

I close my notepad and prepare to go for a run.

Ménage à trois

(Lucy)

'Ping'

> *Hi Lucy,*
>
> *I'm thinking the idea of a three-way was not yours.*
>
> *I hope you don't mind me contacting you out of the blue. If you would like to meet for a drink, just you and me, I would like that very much.*
>
> *Kirk.*

I had finished my Zumba class, showered and was sat in the leisure centre café. I had ordered a mineral water and a melange of fruit. Usually, it would have been a latte and a chocolate brownie, but the text message had compelled me to make the healthy choice.

Hi Kirk,

I'm very sorry that Becky did that. I was so embarrassed. Meeting again would be lovely. I'm free tomorrow night.

Lucy x

The Chicago way

(Kirk)

She left me waiting long enough for a reply I thought, good for her. It's a refreshing change for a girl not too be too eager.

Lucy seems to be more confident; I like that about her.

We had agreed to go to a cocktail bar called Ma Baker's in a town called Halifax.

I knew of Halifax, I'd been to a number of gigs at the Piece Hall, and other than the quite spectacular venue, I'd not thought much of the rest of the town. Apparently, Halifax had been an affluent major mill town in the past and in the 1980's and 90's was quite the destination for partygoers.

They had more pubs per square mile than anywhere in Europe and it was the place to go for hen and stag dos. The Coliseum Nightclub had legendary status and used to feature on the Hitman and Her show; Pete Waterman and Michaela Strachan's live TV broadcasts in the early hours of Sunday mornings.

Coachloads of people used to arrive in their hundreds on Thursday, Friday, Saturday and Sunday nights.

Not anymore.

The town looks like it's had some hard times since, Ma Baker's however was opulent and glitzy in comparison to the rest of the dreary town.

I'd agreed to meet her outside the old ABC cinema building that is now a bar come nightclub, I was pleased that she'd arrived on time.

On entering the bar, it was clear that this was a successful business, beautifully decorated to the highest specifications, glittery chandeliers hung from ceilings, mirrored walls made the place seem larger and grander. Subtle lighting and plush seating in booths on two floors, created a fabulous cocktail bar feel, we could have stepped back into the nineteen twenties and nineteen thirties of the art deco scene.

The theme of the bar was that of a speakeasy during the prohibition era, the staff were dressed as I would have expected staff to dress in the secret drinking dens of a gangster ruled Chicago.

The cocktail bar was managed by a mother and daughter team, and they were the perfect hosts. Lucy ordered a porn star martini; I believe she was playing it safe with a cocktail that she knew. There was an extensive menu with many cocktails neither of us have heard of. All bespoke cocktails created by the daughter of the team.

We learned that these inventions were advertised on their Facebook page only for the recipes to be stolen by a tik-toking influencer who plagiarised them as her own. You can't copywrite cocktails apparently.

As we took our seats in the booth, Lucy put her hand on my arm and apologised for not telling me about her boyfriend while we were in Amsterdam, who was no longer her boyfriend.

They were not planning to be engaged, that was a fabrication by Becky, probably to attempt to have me for herself, Lucy had surmised.

She said that she'd been contemplating splitting up with Dale, before she went to Amsterdam but didn't want him to think that she was dumping him so she could meet someone on her trip. Ironically, she'd done just that with me.

The breakup had been amicable, to a degree, he'd wanted to know if there was someone else. She'd said no but admitted that her head had been turned. It turned out that Dale had also had his head turned with a girl in his office and although they had not been on a date together, they'd met for drinks after work.

Lucy said that this revelation had confirmed to her that her decision was the right call.

In fact, she'd seen Dale and the girl together a couple of times, Halifax is not a big town.

She'd not been able to call or text me, because she didn't have my number or any other way of contacting me, so she was glad that I'd made contact.

After a very pleasant evening I drove her home, walked her to the door, and gave her a gentle kiss on the cheek before turning to return to my car. Well played I said to myself, very cool.

Almost as soon as I started to walk away, I heard footsteps running behind me.

"You have to come in as meet my mum and dad, they're insisting" Lucy said.

This turned bad quickly.

Kill me now!

(Lucy)

OMG, oh my god, my parents are so embarrassing.

Dad is asking far too many questions.

Where do you work?

Nice car, lease or finance?

Do you own your own place, in that there Leeds? As if Leeds was a dirty word.

He might as well have said, 'I'm going to interrogate you for ten minutes so I can decide if you are good enough to date my daughter'.

At least his approach was not as overt, as Mum's.

Oh, aren't you a strapping lad?

Do you go to the gym?

Would you like a cup of tea? And a biscuit maybe, for a 'special' guest. Special emphasised.

She doesn't bring many men friends back to see us, not like you anyway.

Mum the flirt and Dad the nightmare. Kill me now.

Kirk though, he's so at ease, respectful; kind to both my parents, when I could quite happily take a bat to them. I don't mean that, but they infuriate me.

After he finished his cup of tea he says.

"I must go, I have football in the morning. I need my sleep these days Mrs … I've just realised, I don't know Lucy's last name!"

"It's Campbell, but you can call me Femi" says Mum.

"I'm Akoni, people call me Tony" says my dad.

"Of course. Femi, Tony, it's been a real pleasure meeting you" Kirk says as he makes to leave.

As he drives away, the three of us waving him off, my mum lets out a scream and starts to jump up and down like a child that has had too much sugar.

"Wow girl" she exclaims "What a catch, you've hit the jackpot!" mums shrieks.

Dad sits in his chair with a weird smile on his face.

"I will take a whiskey, then to bed Fem" he says.

I excuse myself and head to bed, thinking of Kirk and the feelings he has left stirring in me.

Big Dog

(Kirk)

"You're too close, give him a yard Goldie!" I scream at our right back, Glover.

Their left-winger has speed, he wants Goldie to be touch tight with him so that he can turn and use his pace to get round and away. He's taking the piss.

Not with my defence he isn't.

Their coaching staff and subs are roasting Goldie.

"Easy day for you, Denny. He's got no pace and built like Barbie" are the calls from their touchline.

I can see he's rattled.

"Goldie, come inside me, play centre half for a minute or two" I instruct him

Their number eleven gets the ball at his feet, turns quickly, fakes to come inside me, then flicks the ball past my right-hand side with his left foot and sprints into the space behind me.

His team mates on the touchline cheer him on.

"You can beat that big old dog" I hear one of them shout.

I'm no slouch though; I can move for a big fella.

'Crunch' man and ball together.

My tradesman tackle, sliding in from the side, taking the ball first and then leaving my kneecap to connect with the side of his knee on the follow through.

I'm up quickly, reorganising the defence for the throw in. I order Goldie to go back to his right-back position having dished out a footballing lesson to their cocky winger.

The whistle blows to halt play, for an injury. Their number eleven needs treatment, he hobbles off, his match is over for today and silence from their mob on the sideline.

Not in my house, Bradford Lions.

"This is Big Dog's House" Goldie shouts to the side line.

Woofs and howls echo around the pitch from our teammates, followed by laughter from both touchlines.

That's the thing about football, it's tribal, but there is a mutual respect. You can dish it out, but you must be able to take it. The Lions of Bradford showed that they could do just that.

To be fair to them, the Bradford side were a good team, strong, physical and quick.

We won the game one goal to nil, a brilliantly taken free kick from Robbo, curled with pace over the wall, with the keeper guarding the opposite side of the goal. He made a great effort to get across, but the power and accuracy was exceptional, right in the stanchion.

Both sets of players congratulated each other on a very sporting and difficult game.

After we showered, we met up again in the bar afterwards, exchanged man of the match award and had a few drinks together.

Robbo was the man of the match voted by them, I thought I'd done enough to be honest, but Robbo's goal was stunning, and I had injured one of their players, to be fair, which probably influenced the votes against me.

We gave the award to their number eleven, and it wasn't a pity award either. Until the moment I'd knocked him in the air he had been a real thorn in our side.

As usual the drinks and football chat were going to continue late into the night, but I was going to excuse myself quietly.

I waited until the drinking games started and slipped unnoticed out of the side door into the car park.

In the car I called Lucy, I picked her up at 7pm, a bottle of scotch for her dad and flowers and chocolates for flirty Femi.

I asked them both if it was OK with them if she stayed at my house, separate rooms of course. There were no protests, Femi was assorting the flowers in a vase and Tony was admiring his whiskey.

Smooth operator

(Kirk)

Lucy didn't say very much on the thirty-minute car journey from her parents to my house, she just had a satisfied smile on her face while she hummed along to the music on the radio.

Absolute 80s is not to everyone's taste, but I've always been a fan of the 80's music era.

It wasn't until we had turned off the M621 onto the ring road that she spoke at all.

"Oh, I forgot to ask, how was the football today? Did you win?"

"Yes, we did, that's three wins out of three without conceding a goal yet this season, we're top of the league with 9 points, 2 points clear of our closest rivals" was my reply.

I looked across at her and realised she was wanting a yes or a no answer.

As we pulled onto the drive alongside my other car, she asked if I lived alone. A reasonable question on seeing another car on the driveway.

"Yes, that's my weekend car" I said.

"It is the weekend" she replied, and we both laughed.

"Ok smart arse" I said. "That's my fun car".

It was usually in my double-garage, but I'd left it out on purpose.

"It's a 1985, Ford Escort RS Turbo Mk1, just like the one Princess Diana owned" I said.

"Hers was black though", mine being bright red.

"80's car, 80's music, I'm surprised you don't have a mullet hairstyle" she said, with a hint of sarcasm and a smirk.

Showing off has not paid off I thought, but I liked the fact that she wasn't impressed by material things. I do love my car though.

I may have to wait to show her my Classic VW SO40 Camper van, it's a very sexy turquoise, teal colour. It's probably worth more than both my Polestar 2, and the Escort combined.

I don't care about its financial value; it provides me with immense pleasure and has a healing effect on my soul.

I can't pretend that I'm not on full show off mode, but materialist things don't do it for her. That's more than fine with me. I hope to impress her with my culinary skills and domestic prowess.

I surprise myself that I want to impress her, but I suddenly realise that she is the one for me. I'm now off the market.

Not that I was ever on the market.

Am I going to stop escorting, yes, I think I will, if she wants to take the next step.

I pour her a glass of wine, a nice little Argentinian Malbec from Aldi that Helen

McGinn promoted on Saturday Kitchen, which complimented a dish made by the very attractive Nadiya Hussain, similar to my dish this evening.

I tell her that she's free to take herself on a tour of the house if she'd like. I give her the directions to the spare room, where I've left her a towel on the bed. She can leave her bags there.

I could do the chivalrous duty and carry the bags up myself, but I'm leaving her to decide whether she puts her bag in the spare room or my room.

While she's roaming round the house, I set about preparing the meal.

Some of it I prepared last night, and because I didn't want to be in the kitchen all night most of it only needs a little preparation and cooking.

I've made a trio of amuse bouchée to start us off and give time to make the starter. The trio consists of a spicy tomato and basil velouté, a tomato and mozzarella bruschetta and a crab croquette, served on 3 individual oriental spoons on a slate board. Very flash.

While we enjoy those, she sits at the breakfast bar opposite my cooking station as I pan fry half a dozen king scallops. When perfectly caramelised, I place three each on plate on top of a smear of pea puree with peas shoot garnish and a crispy Parma ham shard.

So far so good, some more wine and a bit of soft background music, that she chose. Sade Adu, I approve of her choice.

I set about pan frying two succulent filet steaks in butter, and warm through the wild garlic mushrooms. The jumbo chips are cooked for a third time for optimum crispness, and we are ready to serve alongside a simple salad.

In my haste I neglect to ask her how she wanted her steak cooking; they are rare but well rested, so the meat is tender.

"Compliments to the Chef" she says "Please do tell him for me" she laughs.

I chortle too eagerly.

"How did Chef know that I like my steak rare?" she adds.

"It's the only way to eat fillet steak" I reply, hoping for a reprieve.

"You are not wrong" she concludes.

After dinner I suggest that we take the rest of the bottle of wine through to the sitting room.

She looks a little confused, I guess that she was expecting a dessert. So, I ask whether she has a sweet tooth and tell her that I have made a dessert for later and a cheese board, that we can take in the sitting room.

She asks why we're having cheese before dessert; I reply that it depends on where you are as to what order you have a cheese board and dessert. The French way is to have cheese after the main and then dessert to finish. But the British way is to eat the pudding first and have cheese last with port or spirits or both.

Lucy opted for the British way and request a small glass of port, and whatever spirit I was having and whether she could have a Gaelic coffee to conclude.

I was no longer showing off, she was enjoying being pampered.

What's the story morning glory.

(Lucy)

I had not put my overnight bag in the spare room, in fact to make a clear statement I had placed my toiletry bag in Kirk's ensuite and my toothbrush next to his.

I had laid the sexiest negligee I owned across one side of the bed, claiming it as my own. Kirk could be in no doubt that I intended to spend the night with him.

As we shared a glass of whiskey I fell into his arms, and he held me close. His body was solid, and I yearned to touch it, instead we just held each other and fell asleep.

I was woken gently and Kirk led me to the bedroom. I was disappointed with myself because I had designs on a more physical end to the evening.

Kirk was the perfect gent, he gave me the use of the bedroom first, so I was able to dress for bed, freshen up and brush my teeth. He used the main bathroom and knocked to gain permission to enter his own bedroom.

I was already in bed, and he joined me. He was wearing a pair of sweatpants, so I guessed that he did not own pyjamas. But his top half was exposed, and what a top half it was, sculptured, muscular, hairy, defined, and impressive.

He slid into his side of the bed, scooped me into an embrace which gave me licence to touch his body. I suddenly didn't feel so sleepy.

He kissed me in a goodnight kind of way, and I kissed him back in a come and take me way.

The alcohol had given me a bit of bravado, so I allowed my hand to wander inside his trousers, I was flattered to find that he was semi aroused, but shocked at his size. My fingers could not meet around his girth, and it was continuing to grow. My thumb knuckle rubbed against his belly button, but his shaft continued further up his abdomen.

I decided in an instant that I was going to venture south to get a closer look. I kissed his neck, his incredible and hairy chest, his stomach and there it was, his impressive cock was stood to attention and enormous.

I struggled to take it in my mouth but managed it, I kiss, lick and massage it, using all my tricks and techniques, paying special attention to the ball area.

I was fully engrossed and could have continued, but Kirk took control and had begun massaging me, his hand was inside my nightwear and expertly rubbing my clitoris, with outstanding competency. As he did, I kept a hold on his throbbing cock and orgasmed uncontrollably. His technique was unparalleled, and I held him tightly and fell asleep once more.

I awoke in the morning a little embarrassed, not that we had engaged in some foreplay or that I'd had an orgasm, but that I'd not reciprocated. I'm not a selfish lover.

I decide that I was going to make amends, so I woke him with kisses, stroked his magnificent cock and then lowered myself onto him.

I wished that I'd had a little bit of pre fun first, because taking something so large without foreplay was a challenge, but I was pleased that I was in the position of control.

The advantage was temporary, Kirk lifted me effortlessly and rolled me over and took control, the best I ever had, or ever would have.

Agoraphillia
(Rosie)

It's not my first time in York, I've had a few girls' nights out in what has been voted as the best night out two years in succession.

I recall a particularly memorable snog, in the House of Trembling Madness pub in the past, he had me trembling that's for sure. That snog led to a short walk to the York Museum Gardens and alfresco sex. Eager, lustful and selfish sex, up against a wall at first and then bending me over a bench, I came first and second, then him, all within a matter of moments and back to the pub with our brief absence unnoticed.

The thought of him gave me another shudder.

I'd never been to York on business though, this time I'm fixing a meeting between two football hooligan captains, one from York City and one from Leeds Utd.

York City fans had stopped in Leeds after an away match at a team from Greater Manchester last season and their fans had got a bit carried away. A little scuffle in a bar turned into a huge bar fight culminating in the York Nomad Society, York City's hooligan firm, smashing up the bar and injuring a number of customers.

The bar was owned by a former Leeds Service Crew top boy, and there was a call for blood.

There had been apologies and discussions on social media but rather than calming things down, it had escalated as fans from both sides added their opinion.

In the end a York businessman, anonymously, offered to pay for any damage and also to broker a truce, this is where I come in.

It's believed that the businessman's son, was one of the main culprits, but that is rumour.

What is not a rumour is that part of the deal is the surrender of the CCTV footage, from the pub and a signed agreement that copies and or images are not taken and used later.

Once the two captains are talking, I will depart, this is not my usual cup of tea, I'll leave this one with the Vlad's.

Leeds is only thirty to forty-five minutes away depending on the A64, York-Leeds Road, I'm thinking I might visit a certain pawn shop in Leeds.

Soft Pawn

(Kirk)

My pawn shop is closed on Sundays and Mondays, it's closed most days if I'm honest, but the sign on the door and the website says trading is:

Tuesday, Wednesday, Friday	09:00-17:00
Thursday	09:00-19:00
Saturday	09:00-12:00

So today, Lucy and I will be having a leisurely morning in bed, a drive to the coast, Scarborough probably. Fish and chips and ice-cream by the sea and back to Halifax, early evening.

I think we should pick up a Chinese takeaway to share with Tony and Femi, when I take Lucy back home.

Grandad's Watch

(Kirk)

'ping'

> *Mr McDonnel, there's been a lady round here today looking for you.*
>
> *Very pretty lady, if I do say so, but none of my business.*
>
> *She says she is looking to pawn a watch, but I did not see a watch.*
>
> *She doesn't look like the type to be pawning Grandad's watch, if you know what I mean.*
>
> *She gave me her card. Rosie Sparx is her name.*
>
> *Grace x*

How many times do I have to ask you to call me Kirk? I know you do it on purpose, but I like you being a bit cheeky.

I was going to reply telling Grace to concentrate on her Photography studies instead of being nosey, or I'll increase her rent. But I don't. She's a good student, I imagine, and she's a good tenant.

I've turned a blind eye to her converting the unoccupied flat into her photography dark room. She tells me every now and then that she's been in there to check everything is OK, has done a bit of cleaning, sometimes that she has put the heating on to stop the place becoming damp and mouldy. I suppose if I notice that the electricity has been used in that flat, then she's provided a perfectly plausible explanation in advance.

We both know that we both know what is going on. I've no intention of renting the flat to anyone else and she could not afford to rent both flats, even on the next to nothing rent that I'm charging her.

Sometimes it's easier just to let things be.

I have CCTV outside the building, but I also have Grace. The advantage of Grace is that I get an instant text, without having to trawl through CCTV.

But I skirt around the important revelation, why is the fixer snooping around my pawn shop? and not covertly either. And what is the significance of the watch?

I know that there must be a message there about the watch, but it's lost on me. The watch is a clue to something.

I don't have time to think about it too much, it's date night. Wow, I haven't said that in a while.

Scarbs

(Kirk)

Today started surprisingly, my morning glory was taken advantage of, and it felt good.

While Lucy showered, I made breakfast, nothing spectacular, just a little something I picked up in New York.

I fry onion, green pepper, mushrooms and bacon and put to one side. Then I slightly undercook a 3-egg omelette and add the fried ingredients as a filling. Once the omelette is folded it's wrapped in a tortilla and fried once more. Et voila.

We shared half each and a pot of hot strong coffee in the orangery overlooking my impressive garden. Showing off again.

We decided to take the RS Turbo to Scarborough, which was an inspired choice, driving that car is just cracking good fun, and it turns heads.

It was reasonably sunny day although there was a breeze from the sea, and after a welcome walk along the seafront it was time to partake in some fish and chips.

I was surprised that Lucy hadn't visited the east coast before, being from the farthest west of Yorkshire the west coast was more convenient.

We sat on the steps leading to the beach, shoes off to feel the sand between our toes and ate our fish and chip lunch eagerly. Lucy insisted on lunch being her treat and ordered a fish each, haddock of course, we are not heathens that eat fried cod. Skin on as is the way on the coast and we shared some chips and gravy.

We managed to polish it off without seagulls bothering us too much, and we had room for an ice cream as we walked back to the car along the beach. I chose rum and raisin, Lucy had mint choc chip with a waffle cone.

As we neared the car, we were treated to an impromptu flyby of classic aeroplanes heading either to or from an airshow. Lucy said she recognised a Halifax bomber fly overhead. I had to take her word for it, she seemed certain, and I had no reason to doubt her. It was a very impressive looking plane and very noisy. It didn't move particularly fast, and I could see why the bombers of World War Two required the protection of the nimble spitfire fighter aircraft.

We were about to call it a day and venture back to West Yorkshire, but instead we were enticed by the lights and sounds of the games arcade. We both had the same addiction to 2p machines, and for little under twenty quid we won a mini snow globe, a refresher sweet, a book of vampire stick-on tattoos, a hello kitty comb and a Paddington key ring.

I tried not to be too perturbed that the snow globe was attached to my dashboard with chewed chewing gum, my new keyring was that of Paddington Bear and my left arm was adorned with temporary vampire tattoos, mostly upside-down, which pleased Lucy immensely. I didn't get close to the refresher chew.

The two-hour plus car journey to Lucy's parent's house was entertaining, Absolute 80's on the radio as we played guess the intro, guess the song and the artist. I'm surprised at her knowledge of 80's popular music.

We stop at the Tian Tian Chinese takeout, near Lucy's parents' home and the favourite take away of her Mum and Dad. Sweet and sour chicken with boiled rice for Femi, roast pork with garlic and chilli sauce for Tony, with chips. Prawn chow mein for Lucy and special curry and noodles for me. We order half a crispy aromatic duck and some spring rolls and barbeque spareribs to share.

We arrive at Lucy's parents with the Chinese meal and a bottle of sauvignon blanc.

The meal was pleasant, Lucy was clearly feeling uncomfortable, but I enjoyed the interaction with Tony and Femi. Not so enjoyable was the touchy-feely hands of Femi. I decide that I will sit opposite her in future.

Femi offers me the choice to stay on the couch, but I make a very feeble excuse and leave.

I tell Lucy, that I'll call her later, and I will. I like her very much.

Battle Royal

(Kirk)

The friendliest person I know, is the florist that rents a space in my little row of shops. Vicky to her friends and family, but I call her by her Sunday name, Victoria.

I don't like to get too familiar, we flirt a bit, but she is married. Happily, it would seem. If she were not, that would be another matter, she is very attractive and there is something extra special, that I can't put my finger on. But I'd like to.

I was calling in today to buy flowers for Lucy, I wish I'd taken my trade elsewhere.

Far too many questions.

"Who's the lucky lady?"

"How many dates has it been? Just to help me with the flowers for the arrangement".

"You don't want to look too eager, do you Kirk?"

Her shop is open less than mine, she has such a hectic social life, and the shop is more of a hobby.

Victoria and her husband Craig are retired. They're only in their fifties but retired. They both had professional jobs and a big family and were expecting to have to work until they were approaching seventy, but then Craig had a bit of a lottery win. Not the jackpot, or that's the story as Victoria tells it, but enough to mean that they don't have to work and can maintain their five holidays a year lifestyle.

I tell you, she's abroad more often than she's in England.

Victoria had always wanted a little shop, hobby, so this place is ideal for her. Craig plays golf, five times a week with his mate Andy. Andy left his accountancy job to be Craig and Victoria's Business Manager and

Accountant, the reality being that he doesn't have to work so he can golf with Craig.

Grace, the Photography Student, from the flat above works part time for Victoria, mostly Saturday's but anytime she can cover for Victoria so she can 'nip out', which is frequent and often.

The two of them together are a nightmare, a comedy double act, with a sting in the tail.

I'm 6 foot 5 and build like a barn, and they terrify me. Give me a locker room full of football players any day of the week.

Lads dish out a jibe and back off. These two are relentless, aim for the jugular and maintain the pressure point.

If you've seen the WWF Battle Royal, it's a verbal version of that. But to be clear, I would not step in the ring with them either.

She's made a terrific bouquet of flowers for me, not over the top, a nice little bunch of seasonal flowers.

"Not too many men know how to treat a lady these days, Kirk" she says. "Flowers for no reason at all is a beautiful romantic gift that makes a girl feel special".

"Now that will be, twenty-five quid, cash, I don't trust your credit" she scoffs.

A million to one chance

(Rosie)

Pieter was in Edinburgh was my information, which had been unexpected. What was even more surprising is that he had announced himself to the Scottish Capital as his alter-ego, Vander.

His dual identity was known to only Adrianus and I, as far as I was aware. Many local people of Amsterdam knew Pieter as the famous milkshake maker from the Insomnia Coffee Shop, and one or two of his close business associates knew him as Vander. Only those directly involved in either the trafficking of girls or the management of prostitution in Amsterdam knew him by that name, but they did not know he was Pieter.

Outside of Holland he was known as the Dutchman, but he had kept his identities secret for decades.

The names Vander and Dutchman were known throughout Europe, their names would strike peril in people. No one knew who they really were, they were phantoms, feared elusive people that nobody had met, yet their names alone would invoke fear far beyond their capability.

Why would The Dutchman arrive in Scotland to announce himself as not only Pieter but also Vander?

I imagine that The Apparition is also aware that Vander is hunting him and that while assuming the identity of Pieter the barman, in Amsterdam during the goods exchange, Pieter/Vander, knew what he looked like.

Vander, the Dutchman, was starting his hunt in the capital of Scotland for three specific reasons. One, it's the city that The Apparition had claimed to hail from. Two, he has over a hundred girls working for him in Scotland, mainly in Edinburgh and Glasgow and the surrounding area. Thirdly, he has contacts in Edinburgh, and he is aware that The

Apparition was recommended by associates of these in Edinburgh.

He meant business, he intended to make an example of The Apparition, not only was he leading the hunt himself, but he and Adrianus had put out a bounty of one hundred thousand euros for information that would lead to the capture of the Ghost. A further twenty thousand was available if he was apprehended and handed over, alive.

I had extensively searched the birth records in the Edinburgh hospital where Kirk was born, there were no records of twin boys that year. I had no more details to go on other than Kirk had been adopted at birth, his birth parents saw that his identity stayed a secret.

I did not believe that our Kirk McDonnel, was The Apparition, or know whether he had a brother, a twin or whether he knew who The Apparition was, but I had one hundred and twenty thousand reasons to find out.

Look-a-likes are rare, one in tens of thousands, maybe hundreds of thousands. The chances of your Doppelganger turning up in Amsterdam for a drug deal, the very same time you are there to meet a client and play in a charity football match must be a million to one chance.

An extraordinary coincidence, and in my business, coincidences don't happen too often.

You either have a twin brother, Mr Kirk McDonnel, or you have an alter-ego, a Dr Hyde to your Mr Jekyll.

Rosie and Grace

(Grace)

The lady, Rosie Sparx, was it? has left Mr McDonnel, Kirk's establishment, she appears to be carrying an old, tarnished watch.

That must have been the item she wanted to sell him; he mustn't have been interested or the price was too high. I can't imagine she needs the money. Big posh limousine and burly security guards at her disposal. Plus, those clothes, they were not off the rack.

She was in the shop with Kirk for a good thirty minutes, I wonder what the conversation was all about. He's not much for a conversation so it must have been Ms Sparx that was doing all the talking.

"Hi Rosie" I say, "Still have your Grandad's watch?" I add.

"Hmm" she looks startled, and don't think that happens often with this lady.

"I couldn't sell it, Grace, is it? Too sentimental in the end" Rosie adds, regaining her composure, but I don't buy it. Something significant has happened in there.

Her car speeds away and Kirk locks up for the day and speeds off too. Interesting.

Vicky is not at her shop so I cannot gossip with my friend. I head back to my flat to wrestle with my thoughts and find that I have received a letter from Rosie, with instructions and one hundred pounds as an advance.

Part Four

The Thot Plickens

Where there's a Will, there's a way.

(Isla)

"Kyle, I think you want to be a good man, a good husband and a good father" I say, and I genuinely believe it.

"I'm not giving up on us just yet, and not just for the sake of the children" but I don't genuinely mean it.

"So, your request for me to give you fifty thousand pounds as a separation settlement is not accepted" I add, and I can see that he is disappointed.

"The reading of my parents Will is to be tomorrow afternoon, in private as per their instructions. There will be just my father's solicitor and I, with Mr Farquarson's secretary, Betty, as witness" I explain.

"The cash, shares and bonds are expected to be a little over a quarter of a million pounds" I add.

"And then there's the house, which is estimated to be around the million-pound mark. For a quick sale we've been advised that we should look to get eight hundred to eight hundred and fifty thousand."

He shows some interest for the first time in our conversation, he's been edging towards our kitchen door for the past five minutes, staring at his empty coffee mug and trying to find the words to excuse himself.

"You know my parent's feelings about you Kyle" I say as sensitively as I can muster.

"So, Mr Farquarson, has advised that we must be prepared for some conditions of my inheritance" I say, and I reach out to touch his arm, but he pulls away.

"More specifically Kyle, protection from you accessing the money" I add, in a matter-of-fact way.

"Mr Farquarson has indicated that there is likely to be a trustee appointed who will approve any cash advances, but I alone will be permitted to make a request".

"He's suggested that a Mr Castel would be the acting trustee".

"I asked him if my dad had left any provisions for us to upgrade the house, my dad had always said that when he passed that he wanted us to get a bigger house, a family home with room for Maisie and Hamish to play. A garden big enough for Hamish to practice his football or rugby and maybe a stable for Maisie. That was Dad's dream for us" I said. Maybe an old farm I thought.

"Mr Farquarson couldn't tell me but said that my father had often talked about provision for a new house for us. If he were to guess, he would think that we'll be permitted to use the sale of the house to invest in a new family home" I say excitedly.

"The cash however is to be tightly controlled, I'm afraid" I reiterate to conclude the conversation.

Kyle's face reddens and he leaves without saying a word.

Plan A

(Kyle)

Fuck, fuck, fuck, fuck, fuck.

Isla is about to a millionaire, and I won't see a penny.

Who gives a shit that mummy and daddy didn't like me, they are dead, and their money is very much alive and mine in the event of her death. Her father and Mr Farquarson cannot stop that.

Nothing has changed, it's the same game, the stakes have been raised that's all.

Plan A needs a slight tweak that's all.

A million-pound house, eh? I'd not been invited to the house so I wouldn't know. I know it is near the coast but that's about it.

Is he in heaven, is he in hell?

(Vander)

The Apparition is exactly that, nobody knows him, it's as if he never existed before we hired him, and he's vanished into his normal life. All my contacts, and my contacts' contacts have come up with absolutely nothing.

He's the best undercover agent we've ever encountered. Adrianus was contacted by our Mr Apparition via the dark web informing him that a Belarusian drug dealer had designs on moving in on Amsterdam, he had money, power and muscle.

The Apparition was the man with the plan, a real-life Roger 'Verbal' Kint. His plan was simple and slick.

Adrianus had not appraised me of the entire scope of the plan, had he, I might not have played along. My cover as Pieter the barman was perfect for me to be hidden in plain sight.

It was true that I'd not thought much of The Apparition when I'd first seen him in his silly fancy dress and even less when I met him in person in the Insomnia Coffee Shop. I thought him a fool and I thought Adrianus had made a huge mistake, I did not say so.

I'm reminded of the Scarlet Pimpernel character Sir Percival Blakeney, played by Sir Anthony Andrews, he played the fool, a clumsy fop, an aristocratic airhead, but this was an act as he was a brave hero that risked his life to rescue noblemen and women from the guillotine, with cunning plans.

Our Apparition was certainly as elusive as that damned Scarlet Pimpernel.

Adrianus had introduced me to the plan to sell a small quantity of cocaine to the man we knew to be Maksin of Belarus, using the Apparition as a go between rather than one of our own men.

The rationale was that Maksin may guess that he is dealing with us but there would be no link to our business until we were ready to do business, if at all.

Adrianus is very careful who he does business with, he has many important and powerful friends, and he needs to maintain the façade as a respected businessman, which is why he couldn't do business with the notorious Vander, and why my identity as Vander has been a mystery until now.

The plan for Maksin, was for him to receive the best quality product so that he would see that muscling in on our business would take some doing, his product would have to match ours which would reduce profit margins, and we hoped to dissuade him from pitching a tent in Amsterdam.

We were aware that his chosen method of doing business was collaborative rather than aggressive. Adrianus was not closed to the possibility of professional friendship with Maksin, but partnership was not on the cards.

The Apparition presented a plan to create a scenario whereby a partnership would be impossible but without causing a disagreement between the two families. In addition, there was a plan to set up some tension which would send him back to his homeland.

I was not privy to either part of the plan. We were to follow the Apparition's instructions, and he would take away the threat of the Volvov's.

He correctly predicted that Maksin would have him followed, so he would wear a disguise.

The first part of the plan would be for Adrianus to tell him to ditch the disguise. That would be the confirmation to The Apparition that the deal was on.

Part two, would see him losing the tail Maksin had on him and ditching his disguise would allow him to do that.

We were not expecting him to play the fool, nor were we prepared for his double cross.

His attack on one of my girls was a deliberate act to draw tension between Adrianus and Maksin, particularly Maksin.

We didn't know that this was his plan, and it caught us cold. He knew that the manor of the violent attack would be enough to render any business deal between the families impossible, but he had the intuition to realise that the families would come together to hunt him down, this guy was good.

He'd planned his escape meticulously, including anticipating that he would be tracked or picked up on the train.

Having Maksin and his men look incompetent ensured that Maksin would leave Amsterdam without a deal.

Murdering Maksin's favourite niece in Lille, would end any possibility of him returning to Amsterdam. By now Maksin would conclude that his man The Apparition, was in fact

Adrianus' man and that the death of his niece was a warning.

The only error that The Apparition made was underestimating Pieter the barman and not realising that Adrianus and Vander are business associates.

The choice of girl was deliberate, any girl would not have worked. It had to be a girl owned by Vander that would bring about the series of events that followed.

Arriving at Edinburgh, announcing myself as Vander and not the Dutchman had not brought The Apparition out of hiding. Revealing that Pieter and Vander are the same person, and connected to Adrianus has not enticed him out from his cover.

The Apparition has still not been paid in full; we had anticipated that my arrival in Scotland would provoke him to come after me.

We were not convinced that he lived in Edinburgh, but we were sure that he was in

Scotland, and we believed that he had links Edinburgh.

Any guesswork however educated and calculated had returned zero results, so my journey was at an end. My flight was booked for tomorrow lunchtime, information gathered, Scotland is still cold and wet.

Speak of the Devil
(Kyle)

I'd seen the Russian goons, and a stunning petite woman leave Scotland, destination London via Yorkshire.

They'd not paid me any attention as they were escorted to their waiting car, why would anyone pay attention to a workman in his overalls looking at the drains?

Their driver had shared a cigarette break with the footman if The Balmoral and disclosed that they were from Mayfair in London, the lady of the house owns the property, and her security and driver live on site along with a husband-and-wife couple who are the butler and the cook and also housekeepers.

They were stopping over at the Grand Hotel in York for two nights, and he is hoping to get home in time for the Chelsea home match.

As they left, there was another arrival. Word spread fast that a man known as the Dutchman was in town and that he was a dangerous individual. He was visiting the capital to check on his girls, which had sent fear throughout the prostitution community in Edinburgh.

You would not guess that prostitution is illegal in Edinburgh, there are sex clubs, brothels, escort agencies and literally hundreds of prostitutes operating in just about every part of the city.

Most people in the city have never met the Dutchman, and many people doubted that such a man existed. Many of the working girls believed that he was a fictitious character, a phantom meant to create fear and compliance.

The greatest trick the devil ever pulled was convincing the world that he did not exist. Is the famous line from a famous movie.

The devil had arrived, and I was keen to investigate.

It didn't take much doing, he announced himself to the heads of some of the main families in both the west and east of the city, displaying respect to both the catholic and protestant factions of our fractured city.

He had introduced himself as Pieter and as Vander and there ended my ignorance as to who Adrianus had referred to in his message. Vander, AKA the Dutchman was a trafficker of girls, and a pimp. I guessed that the girl I visited in Amsterdam was one of his girls and realised that I had met him in a coffee shop there called Insomnia, Pieter. Everything makes sense now, Adrianus and Pieter work together, Adrianus runs drugs, Pieter's alter ego, Vander, runs the girls.

Pieter's arrival in Edinburgh is not to check on his girls, he is looking for me.

I'm not worried, I'm a nobody in my city, no one would believe that Kyle is anything other than a bit of a loser, unable to mastermind such a job. Even those closest to me would doubt that I've ever left Scotland.

Nevertheless, I will keep vigilant, but I don't have time to waste glancing over my shoulder. I have much to do.

Time to grieve.
(Isla)

Maisie and Hamish are staying with Kyle's parents for few days, I laid it on thick that the work situation was meaning long hours and that I was upset and anxious about the reading of the Will.

They had agreed without question. They said that the children should not be exposed to my grieving and Kyle would support me. Of course he will, I thought.

I expect a reaction from Kyle, and not in a positive way, he'll want to know how he can get his hands on my inheritance, what I don't know is how desperate he is. He's always in debt to someone, and generally not very nice people, but that is not my concern this time. I'm not bailing him out anymore.

Trigger happy.

(Kirk)

The doorman briefing is at the Tron on Hunter Square, no role calls as it's assumed that none of us are too stupid not to show up on time. We get our pubs allocated and nightclubs for those on all night duties.

I'm with Duncan, known as Big Dunc, Teddy AKA Bear and Davie. Duncan is a big fella, a friendly fella and a bloody good doorman, he's an old school pal of Isla and he has my back I'm told.

Bear is scary as fuck, Grizzly is another name he goes by, just not to his face. Davie doesn't belong on the doors but is a close find of Bear and Dunc, so he's accepted, and they have his back.

We are assigned to working the doors of The Worlds End pub, and later at The Liquid Room.

My nickname is Trigger, after the only fools and horses' character, only Kyle had omitted that detail from the brief.

"What's fucking up with you tonight, Trig?" Says Bear.

"We've had a whisper that there will be some trouble tonight, I can't be watching out for you Trigger" He barks, or is it a grizzly growl?

"I'm fine, I just need a line" I reply, thinking that is something Kyle would have said.

"Davie give this stiff some happy dust, for fucks sack" another growl from the Bear as he stomps off.

"One bag of Peruvian marching powder my friend" says Davie, tossing me a small plastic resealable pouch.

I've passed the first test, I think.

"Dunc, you can partner this soppy sod on the front door, Davie and I will do the bar and toilets" Shouts Teddy.

"ID everyone, any apprehended contraband is passed to me, no questions. We'll split at the end of the night as usual. Dunc and I will have cash equivalent, you junkies can keep the pharmaceuticals" Bear confirms.

I follow the lads lead.

"Aye" says Big Dunc

"Aye" says Davie, taking a sniff.

"Aye Boss" I say.

"Boss? Are you arf yer heed? Are you proper fucked behind those sunglasses?" he yells.

I'm hoping he doesn't tell me to take off the glasses or the plan could be blown.

"Just being daft Bear" I say with a shrug.

"Cut it out you prick" he tells me.

"Dunc keep an eye on this melt, any fuck ups tonight and it's on you".

"I'm not having Jimmy paying me a visit tomorrow lunchtime spoiling my Sunday

Dinner" Bear growls and he disappears into the bar area.

"Really Trigger?" Dunc says to me.

"Are you deliberately trying to fuck this up?"

Date Night

(Isla)

"This is lovely Kyle; I thought you had forgotten our date night" I said.

"Especially following the news from the reading of the Will" I added.

Kyle had responded calmly, he knew that he wouldn't benefit from my parents Will, that was no surprise he said. Yes, he had wanted money to pay off some debts, but he'd come to an arrangement with them.

He was happy that I'd given him a second chance in our marriage, that he probably didn't deserve, he promised that he'd give it his all and if it didn't work out at least we could say we did our best.

"A least we can say we gave it a go, Isle's" he said, and Kyle hadn't called me Isle's in years.

He did seem genuinely sincere, and surprisingly charming. I don't remember him being charming, but I suppose he must have been at some point, the early days at least.

Curtains Up

(Kyle)

"I have a surprise for you before the theatre" I tell Isle's.

We drive southeast towards Berwick-upon-Tweed, playing name that song, the artist and the year on the radio, a point for each and five points if you get all three. Our name is the buzzer.

Neither of us are very good, we sing along to the songs mostly and she googles the answers, and we laugh hysterically.

Isla doesn't question where we are heading, nor does she question whether we'll be late for the theatre. The girl I met long ago had returned, footloose and fancy free, not a care in the world. Just like when we first met, before children and a mortgage.

We pull into the driveway of a huge, detached house, she looks puzzled.

"Come on" I say, "This could be our new home, a new start".

The house is impressive, I can see that she is suitably impressed too.

"Could we" she says "Really, Kirk, could we?"

"It has gardens and a stable" I say.

"Just like Daddy wanted for us" she says excitedly.

It has a wine cellar.

(Kyle)

We start on the first floor, in the main bedroom, it's impressively large with an ensuite bathroom accessed from two doors, his and hers. There are dressing rooms on either side of the bathroom, one significantly bigger than the other and I guess that's the 'her' side of the room.

French doors lead onto a large balcony that overlooks the rear of the property, and I image that we could watch Hamish and Maisie play from here, it's too dark to see the garden or the stables, but I can imagine for now.

Isla is happy, and I don't speak for fear of ruining the moment.

There are rooms for Hamish and Maisie with a shared bathroom and a guest bedroom also with an ensuite.

"My parents could stay here and babysit" I say to Isla, and she agrees that would be convenient.

We ascend the impressive staircase that leads us down to the hall and the front doors. To the left there is a living room that leads to a sitting room, or it could be a TV room, there is another set of French doors leading out to the back and another door that leads to the kitchen diner that stretches across the back of the house.

At the right of the staircase there is a study at the front of the house and dining room that leads to the kitchen at the back of the house and back around to the sitting room.

At the side of the kitchen there is a downstairs bathroom, a shower room, a boot room and a utility room in a side extension that lead to the stables.

"It's perfect" I say.

"OK, Kyle, how did you find this place?" Isla asks me.

"It's not on the market yet" I tell her.

"Big Dunc knows the solicitor of the guy that's selling It" I say.

"If we, if you, make an offer Duncan thinks we can stop it being put up for sale".

"Six hundred and fifty thousand to seven hundred thousand pounds is what they are looking for" I whisper.

"Didn't you say that your parents' house could be sold quickly for around eight hundred thousand?" I ask her.

"With your inheritance you could buy this house Isla"

"Our family home, just like your father wanted for you, it's perfect for us" I say as I hold her close, and she hugs me too, but it feels like the hug from a friend.

"Don't say anything yet, there is another surprise" I tell her.

We head down into the cellar via a door at the side if the kitchen that leads underneath the main staircase.

"There is a wine cellar or a whiskey cellar" I tell her.

We enter room, larger than I expected, red brick walls and ceiling.

"And through that door there is a gym, sauna and a small swimming pool" I say to Isla, and I point to a door on the far side of the cellar.

Solitary

(Isla)

I'm urged by Kyle to go through the door first to see the magnificent leisure facility.

As I enter, I feel a strong push in my back thrusting me forward and I stumble to the floor.

It takes me a moment for my eyes to adjust to the darkness, and I see that I'm in a small room with a mattress on the floor and a wooden chair in the corner. Is this to be my prison cell?

"Kyle, what's going on" I shout.

"Let me out of here" I beg.

"Quiet, let me think" I hear him say.

"You're going to kill me aren't you Kyle, for the money?" I say and burst into tears.

Smooth Criminal

(Kyle)

I pretend to be a nobody, a petty criminal at best, low level drug dealer and it works.

The reality is that I'm an assassin for hire, a sophisticated smoother type of criminal, a competent operator that blends in, a master of disguise, a ghost.

I don't advertise myself as a killer, a hitman, but I provide that service. Killing does not provide me with any remorse but killing the mother of my children is more difficult that I had anticipated.

How else do I get the money though? Compose yourself man I say to myself and out loud.

"Isla, I'm sorry that I have to do this, I owe a lot of money, you refused to help me while knowing I was in trouble. They would kill me, and you have the means to stop them, but would let them kill me" I yell.

"The only way I get out of this is if you die" I say.

"It must look like an accident" I say in a reluctant tone.

"What about our children Kyle, think about Maisie and Hamish, they don't deserve this" Isla says.

"You would've happily had me die, so I have no regret, you would've taken their father from them, you're a fucking hypocrite" I spit.

"Let me go and I'll give you all the money" Isla screams.

"It's too late for that, this is the only way, I estimate that you have less than four minutes of oxygen before you lose consciousness, your death will be painless".

"Goodbye, Isle's" I say, as I exit the cellar.

Left to die.

(Kyle)

I pause at the door that leads to the kitchen and look back at the door where my wife is dying.

I put on my rubber gloves and ready myself for the nasty bit. I don't need to wipe down any surfaces or handles, I didn't touch anything, I kept my hands in my pockets almost the entire time and allowed Isla to enter rooms first.

The boot of the car is already lined with a plastic sheet, and I have a holdall and ties, ready to take her to her final resting place ready to be found.

Her death will look suspicious, asphyxiation so it will be known that she was killed elsewhere and dumped. The time of death will be established at a time when I have a solid alibi, on the doors at The Worlds End pub with Big Dunk, I'm always working with Big Dunk, and usually Bear and Davie too.

I prop the kitchen door open and move all the obstacles to give me a clear route to the car. I'm going to reverse the car to the front door, car keys in hand I head into the hall and the front of the house.

"Hello, Kyle, or is it Apparition?" says the big Russian.

"This way" says the other one, leading me to the living room.

I recognise them from Maksin's suite in Amsterdam and the Balmoral Hotel in Edinburgh. I wonder if they are with Maksin or the lady.

My exit via the front door is blocked, I know that there is way out through the sitting room and then the kitchen. I saw a key in the French doors, so I just need to delay them slightly by blocking one of the doors between the living room and my new exit route.

I attempt to enter the living room first, but I'm held back by one of the Russians who opens the door and enters himself and disappears inside, I hang back and quickly assess whether I can catch the other Russian off guard and make for the front door, but he's right behind me and eases me through the open doorway.

Stood by the fireplace I see a familiar face.

"Please take a seat" says Pieter, and he points to a wooden stool against the doors of the sitting room. Could this be my chance.

"Let me introduce myself, Kyle, I'm Pieter Van Der Beek. You may know me as Vander. You assaulted one of my girls in Amsterdam and for that you will have to answer" he adds, trying to appear sinister.

I'm not worried about Vander; I can take him. The two Russians are another matter, but if I have to fight for my life, I'm ready.

"You have the wrong man!" I protest as I edge towards the stool, but I don't sit, instead I kneel on it with my left leg.

"You are looking for a man by the name of Kirk McDonnel, I bumped into him by accident outside a pub in Edinburgh, he was asking about Amsterdam, a scary fella" I add.

The Russian's look at each other, they know something.

"You've met him, haven't you?" I say to the Russian pair.

"Yes, we have" says a female voice and in steps the lady I've seen them with at the Balmoral.

"We know Kirk, he works with us" she says.

"Please sit" says Pieter.

I'm not going to sit down unless I'm forced to, the door to the sitting room is slightly ajar, can I get through it and wedge the door shut from the other side. That would give me the time I need to get out of the back doors.

I might not be able to tackle the two Russians, but I wager I can outrun them and lose them in the Scottish countryside.

"I've been set up" I say, "and I think you all know it" I say.

The Russian's both turn to look at their boss lady, and that's my chance.

I thump Pieter hard in the stomach and he goes down in a heap, I dart for the sitting room door and straight into the giant frame of Big Dunc.

"Where the fuck do you think you are going" he says.

Behind him there is Isla, freed from the room, and Kirk.

I slump onto the stool.

One of the Russians makes a move to help Pieter, but he waves them away and straightens up. He's tougher than I gave him credit for.

There is no escape here, I'll take my chance when we get outside. I'll turn on the waterworks and beg and then make a run for it.

"I'm sorry Isle's, I was desperate" I say.

"Dunc, take care of her" I plead.

"Fuck you" Dunc replies.

"No hard feelings Kirk, it wasn't personal, it was too good an opportunity" I say to him, but he doesn't reply.

"Time to go" say Pieter.

The Russians take an arm each and walk me out of the room, the front door and towards the car.

As we approach my car I see another figure, I realise that he's the executioner.

I start to beg for my life, the boot of my car is open, and the holdall is on the floor. The figure is holding what I believe must be my spare car keys, this has been well planned.

I can see the plastic lined boot I had readied for Isla and realise that this is literally my last chance.

I scream and start to cry and beg.

"Isla, please save me!" I cry.

I drop to one knee and push the two Russians away and push off my right leg to start to sprint.

'Bang', I'm struck from behind and collapse to the floor, as my eyes flutter and begin to close I see Pieter holding a cosh, he got his own back.

My House

(Isla)

"It's time for me to go" says Pieter "I have a private jet landing shortly at Borders Gliding Club.

"It's time for us to leave too" Rosie says, "We are not killers, killing is not our business".

"Me too" says Big Dunc, "I need to get back to work".

"Are you, OK?" Dunc asks Isla.

"No, but I will be" she replies.

It's just me and Kirk left in the house.

"Who's is this house" says Kirk.

"My mum and dad's" I say.

"Well, actually, mine as of this morning"

Panic Room

(Kirk)

I never believed Kyle's plea to cover his work duties so he could take Isla to the theatre.

I wasn't going to do it, even for the thousand pounds on offer. But when I met Isla, I agreed to it for two reasons, if he was being genuine, then offering the opportunity for a date night would be a nice thing to do for Isla. If there was an ulterior motive, I would have time to find out what it was. I did not suspect murder though.

When Rosie was sniffing around my pawn shop with a story of a watch, I knew that there was something amiss.

She would not deviate from electronic communication, and the protection of her anonymity if it wasn't for a reason.

I agreed to meet her at my shop to give the appearance of a legitimate proposed sale.

Rosie had told me of the drug deal in Amsterdam involving The Apparition, and the violent rape of one of Vanders girls, and that the perpetrator of both was an almost exact resemblance of me.

I was told that he'd changed his identity and had escaped only to commit a murder in France.

Rosie explained that although she had not believed the villain was me, that she had not discounted that I had a brother, maybe a twin and that I could be an accomplice.

I'd explained to her that I'd been oblivious to any crimes in Amsterdam, but I did tell her about that strange reaction from our physio and the guy in the pub in the pilot outfit. It turns out that this was Kyle.

I told Rosie about my brush with Kyle in Edinburgh, and she told me about the sting they were trying to pull at the Balmoral Hotel.

I had told Rosie of the chance meeting with Isla when I was intending to meet a certain

Irish waitress, and the lovely time that Isla and I had spent together.

Rosie had agreed to contact Adrianus and Vander to explain the plan.

Grace had followed the instructions from Rosie and had met Pieter as he was about to check in for his flight to Amsterdam. The instruction was for him to meet at a property in the Berwick-upon-Tweed area, where he would be greeted by Rosie.

Rosie had visited Isla and appraised her of the plan to catch Kyle in a trap, we had predicted that Isla would be apprehensive, but Rosie would convince her that catching him in a trap was the only way to prove he intended to kill her.

I'd agreed to follow through on my agreement to cover his work shifts.

We were going to rely on Isla recruiting Big Dunc and Mr Farquarson to play their part, a part that they played well.

Mr Farquarson provided a mystery man with keys to Isla's parents family home and spare keys to Kyle's car.

Mr Farquarson had also provided Duncan with the keys to Isla's parents' house and Duncan had provided Kyle with the false information that the house was about to be placed on sale and also the vital part of the plan. That the cellar had a panic room that required power, via a generator, to provide air circulation.

The generator was currently broken, Big Dunc had advised Kyle, and that the room did not open from the inside without the power of the genny.

Dunc had warned Kyle against accidentally locking himself in the room, estimated that he'd have about five minutes of oxygen before he would pass out and ultimately die.

The trap was set, Kyle was provided with both the opportunity and method for his kill.

Duncan had also played the part in The Worlds End; he knew that I was an imposter, but he played along. We had to play that part of the plan, if I hadn't turned up either Bear or Davie would've called Kyle to check where he was and that would have blown the plan out of the water.

Isla needed to trust that we would all be in position when Kyle was to exact his nefarious deed.

We were all at her parents' house before they arrived. The key in the French doors of the kitchen would be the message to Isla that we were all in place.

When they descended the stairs to the cellar we entered through the unlocked French doors and took our positions in the living room and sitting room.

We just needed Kyle to reappear from the cellar alone which he did right on schedule.

The final curtain

(Kirk)

"What will they do with him?" Isla asks me.

"Best not think about it" I reply

"I imagine that it will be quick, painless" I add, being sensitive.

"They don't need to torture him for information or anything like that, it will be efficient" is my opinion.

"Oh, good" she says.

"They will most likely dispose of any evidence, so I don't think his body will be found Isla" I reluctantly state.

There is a long silence and then she bursts into tears.

"What will I tell Maisie and Hamish?" Isla says.

"Rosie and I have talked about that, we have a suggestion, it's a bit unusual, but I do look a lot like their dad"

Part Five
The Last Hangman

Pierrepoint

(Vander)

An alert from the dark web. There was just one message and an attachment from call sign, Pierrepoint.

Very clever I thought, Albert Pierrepoint, executioner, and the last hangman.

The message advised that the message and attachment would expire in one hour, and that the video would erase itself if there was an attempt to download or save it.

The attachment was a video, eighteen minutes long, so I poured myself a double Jenever and settled in.

The image at the start was shaky, the cameraman was placing the camera on a tripod I presumed and was getting the angle and focus right.

The image was dark at first and difficult to make out who the person in front of the screen was, a few additional lights and the view was clear.

Kyle was awakened with a bucket of water thrown at him by huge figure of a man, a man with a frame over 2 meters tall, and in excess 350 pounds, and a scarily dressed individual looking like a horror film character.

Kyle was naked, tied and gagged to a metal chair in a room lined with plastic sheeting. The chair was of a similar design to the alternative pleasure chair that you'd find in an S and M dungeon set up, but this chair was not to be used for pleasure.

As Kyle recognised the reality of the situation, he began to fight at the restraints, but it was hopeless.

His head was held in place inside a half metal helmet which supported the back of his head and neck and prevented him from turning or lifting his head. His head was restrained from moving forwards by two leather straps, one across his forehead and the other across his chin.

His neck was secured in place with a thick leather collar fastened tight with two buckles and in his mouth was filled with a gag with straps around his face, presumably tied at the back.

Both his arms were strapped in three places on the back and the arms of the chair. Just under his armpits and just above his elbow were tied against the back of the chair and his wrists were securely fastened to the chair arm with metal clamps that were padlocked.

There was a huge strap across his chest and one just as impressive across his waist, tied at the front with buckles and padlocked also.

His legs were tied spread wide on two leg supports, just like his arms in three places, upper thigh, under the knee and ankles. The ankles secured with metal clamps and padlocks. His feet were not touching the ground.

All these straps served to negate the need for a seat, and his bottom and genitals were exposed. That was the purpose for this chair of course. The submissive slave would have his or her sexual parts on display for their master to have unrestricted use of.

The purpose of this particular chair set up was torture and Kyle knew it.

The executioner was dressed in filthy green overalls, and an equality squalid brown leather full apron, black rubber sleeve gloves, surgical mask and headscarf and work boots.

I was sure that the attire was for practical purposes, blood splatters and the like, but he could have worn a disposable SOCO suit for that. No, this was for dramatic effect and to scare the shite out of the helpless victim.

Either side of the executioner was his torture tools, surgical trolley to one side, butchers' tools on a wooden block on a table on the other side, Kyle's head positioned to see them in all there shiny and menacing glory.

The executioner stood looking directly at his victim, arms crossed, motionless for almost a minute, but it must have felt to Kyle like ten.

The only sound was Kyle attempting to speak, cry out to beg for his life, the gag muffling these sound, instead deep sharp breaths escaped from his nose in desperation.

The executioner's hands play eenie meenie with the surgical tools, selecting one he then walks behind the chair. Initially he places his gloved hand over the victim's nose and mouth which stifles any sound, with his other hand he pulls back his eyelids and staples them to his forehead and secures them with duct tape.

There were no screams, just despair, his fingers splaying outward with the pain. He knew that not only would he feel the torture, but he would also have to watch the entire process unable to shield the graphic scenes.

The executioner wipes the scalpel across his apron producing a red cross.

"I am Ex" he booms.

X reaches above his head and pulls down a yellow hydraulic 2 button pendant and presses the bottom button. There is a loud clunk and a mechanic whirring of winch and the crunching of steel cables tightening. The machinery tilts the chair backwards into a horizontal position while keeping it from falling back completely.

The sight I'm faced with on the screen is the soles of the man's feet, his exposed arse and genitals. His face is visible in a carefully positioned mirror so that Kyle does not miss the action.

The image is reminiscent of the scene in Law Abiding Citizen, when the character Clyde Shelton, played by Gerrard Butler, tortures and murders the killer of his wife and daughter, Clarence Darby, played by Christian Stolte.

The machinery stops and Kyle is blocked temporarily from view by the hulking figure of X.

Th camera is moved to the left slightly and I can now see the outside of his right leg and the inside of his left leg and his exposed anus that appears to have been greased.

From the right of the screen X brings in another machine which looks like a toolbox on wheels, which he plugs it into the electric mains, I realise it's a fucking machine. From one side of the box protrudes a metal bar to which X has attached an enormous rubber fist.

I wonder to myself whether it has been flown in from Amsterdam.

The machine is wheeled in place and the fist positioned against Kyle's anus, more lubricant is smeared along the length of the fist and more around his anus.

X presses a button on the toolbox, and it starts to murmur, and the bar moves gently forward. The rubber fist is pressing hard against Kyle, but the natural resistance keeps it from penetrating.

X turns a dial and the noise increase, but the dildo does not move. I wonder if the fist is too wide, but the torturer is not perturbed, he sprays more lube of the end of the fist and around Kyle anus and cranks the dial once more.

The machine makes a growling sound like a straining car engine, then thump, the resistance has been broken and the entire fist has vanished inside Kyle, before retracting back so only the fingers of the fist remain inside, then it plunges deep again slow, long strokes, as dictated by the dial.

X shows the dial to the screen, and it's on the number 4, then 5, 6, 7, 8. The fist is hammering away at a terrific speed but not a whimper from Kyle could be heard.

What is the point of this if we cannot tell if he is in pain I thought.

X must have had the same thoughts because he had positioned himself behind Kyle and had loosened and removed the gag.

Kyle was groaning and gargling like a dying animal, trying to speak, 'plea' or 'please' it sounded like but each time he tried to let out a syllable the fist smashed the wind out of him again.

Blood began to show on the arm of the rubber dildo and drip on the floor in a steady stream.

X paused the anal fisting with the arm up to the hilt.

"Kill me" begged Kyle.

X chopped off the toes of his left foot with one slash of a cleaver and Kyle lets out a guttural scream as he passes out.

No More

(Vander)

I pause the horror film and step into the dark night of Amsterdam. Girls are chatting with guys, and couples outside their doorways, the red-light district had returned to normal.

I could not stop this torture, I knew it had taken place many days before, I had to decide whether I needed to see the conclusion to Kyle's demise or whether I was satisfied that justice had been served. He had certainly felt the helplessness and anal rape that his victim had experienced.

The Apparition was no more.

I'd seen enough, I returned to the office and logged off the dark web.

X

(Executioner)

I'd not wanted to engage in the anal torture with the victim, it's not a reputation I wish to have, but the client had paid extremely generously for this specific arrangement.

My reputation has been built on efficient and effective, torture, death and disposal.

Kyle had begged for his life and offered the contents of a safe deposit box in exchange. It was not the money alone that persuaded my leniency; I would not usually surrender my values and principles for money. The use of the fist had disturbed me, I'm an executioner not a defiler. He had also said that he had information for Iron-Bear, that only he knew and that it would go with him to the grave if he did not meet Maksin.

I'd anticipated that the amputation of his toes would pacify the watcher, call sign Voodoo. But I needed to have a contingency.

With another slash of the clever I splashed blood all over the camera and Kyle screamed his final gurling scream and then Kyle is silent and motionless.

I signalled to the viewer that it was over, a moment later I stopped the camera.

Kyle, was no more, Apparition was no more.

Maksin would decide if he could exist with a new identity.

Doppelganger

(Rosie)

Who was the doppelganger? I thought.

Was Kyle, Kirk's doppelganger, or was it the other way around?

Kyle had wished that someone with a similar appearance as his would make themselves known to him, for the purpose of replacing him temporarily, so that he could murder his wife.

If we are to accept that Kirk was the doppelganger, then from the moment that fate brought Kirk into Kyle's life he was doomed.

The ancient myth says that, seeing your doppelganger is considered a terrible omen of misfortune and bad luck. There is little doubt that bad luck befell him when he met Kirk, and his days on the earth were numbered as legend dictates.

Justice has been served Rosie; I said to myself.

Resurrection

(Kyle)

In the Clanlan internet café, Inverness, huddled away in the corner, a bearded trawlerman in his yellow fisherman garbs taps away at the keys and slurps his coffee.

A familiar sight for patrons of the café, he would not draw attention, another foreign fisherman emailing home.

The dark web clicks in and he types.

To: Iron-Bear,

I have information regarding the family that sanctioned the murder of your niece in Lille.

I require extraction from Inverness Airport, today.

From: Mr Arnott McCann

The reply is instant.

The fisherman makes a note inside the lid of his cigarette packet, pours his coffee into the vents of the upright computer and waits. Pop, the screen goes blank, and he is satisfied he has fried the mother board.

The café will not try to fix it, the unit will be destroyed and replaced with a new one, and the evidence of his communication will be lost forever.

He lifts himself out of his seat gingerly, his sea weathered face grimacing, and limps heavily towards the door, and without a word exits the establishment and vanishes.

Epilogue

Dad

(Kirk)

(6 months later)

"Dad, I've missed you," said Maisie.

"I've missed you too, are you taking good care of your mum?" I reply.

"She's got Duncan to take care of her" Maisie, replies doing kiss impressions.

"Dunc" I say, offering my hand.

"Trigger" he says, and winks. Shaking my hand.

"Trigger?" enquires Hamish.

"That's what his mates call him" Big Dunc says. "Do you have a nickname at school?"

"Hammy, or Mish. I don't like either of them" he says.

"It could be worse" his sister chips in "Eh, Duffus?"

"Hello Isla, welcome to Leeds" says Lucy

"Lucy, you look gorgeous" Isla replies, and the girls embrace like old friends.

"It's good to see you" I say to Isla.

"You too" she says.

"OK, introductions blah blah blah" says Maisie "Where's my bedroom dad?"

I show Maisie and Hamish to their rooms and Lucy shows Isla and Duncan to the guest bedroom.

Maisie's bedroom is decorated in soft pastel pinks and peaches, we hoped we'd made it grown up enough for her.

There was a makeup table and a work desk with a laptop. She liked it.

Hamish's room was a Heart of Midlothian shrine, with a gaming area. It was a hit.

So far so good, the story that Isla and I had separated, and I had moved to Leeds had worked. I'd called Maisie and Hamish daily, sometimes video calls, but every day, before they went to bed.

This was the first time we'd seen each other in person so we were all nervous, but it had been good so far.

I'd known that Isla and Duncan were an item shortly after the night in Berwick-upon-Tweed. Neither Duncan nor Lucy knew that we had shared a brief encounter, and there was no merit in them knowing.

Friday night was going to be a relaxed evening, Chinese take away and the kids playing computer games in the snug. That's how it started out, but after a few glasses of wine in, the adults were gaming too.

We were not very good which had Maisie and Hamish in hysterics, but we were all having fun.

The following morning, I took us to an infamous Leeds café for a belly-buster breakfast and then a visit to the Royal Armouries, which was a trip for the kids. They enjoyed it but not as much as the adults.

For the afternoon I had arranged a bit of a curve ball, I had secured tickets for the Leeds Utd v Plymouth Argyle football match, which landed surprisingly well.

Isla and Lucy bonded over wine and a dislike of football. Maisie enjoyed the theatre of it, and the hot dogs.

Hamish decided that Leeds United was his English team and insisted we bought him a football shirt and scarf, which we did.

Saturday evening, we had a lovely meal at Ivy Asia, our waitress Liberty was especially attentive and competent, persuading both Maisie and Hamish to try the sushi.

So far so good.

Sunday morning was going to be a toil.

I cooked a fry up which was a triumph, before we headed to my Sunday morning football match.

I had never been so nervous, we were playing Norton Town, who were top of the league and unbeaten.

We were only 4 points behind them in second place and we had a game in hand.

Maisie and Hamish were expectant, and Isla, Lucy and Dunc revelled in my discomfort.

I need not have been worried; I played well, and we won 4-1. I was a hero to the children.

We had a Yorkshire Sunday Roast and a few drinks, before the Scottish contingent headed home on their train.

We'd agreed that Maisie and Hamish could stay for a week next time, Hamish said only if there was a Leeds United game and Maisie wanted to go to the trampoline park.

Back home, Lucy decided that we were going to have babies of our own.

"Yes, we are" I said, and I led her to the bedroom.

Michael Craig was born in Halifax, West Yorkshire at the end of the 1960s, he now lives in Garforth, Leeds, with His wife Victoria, they have five children.

Printed in Great Britain
by Amazon